# Tricked by Love

Tara Kennedy

# Copyright

This story is a work of fiction. Names, characters, places, and incidents either are products of the author's imagination or are used fictitiously. Any resemblance to actual persons, living or dead, events, or locales is entirely coincidental.

Copyright © 2024 by Tara Kennedy

Copyright © 2023 Excerpt of *Troubled by Love* by Tara Kennedy

Cover image courtesy of appalachianview (deposit photos)

Cover design by Talkapedia Press

All rights reserved. Where such permission is sufficient, the author grants the right to strip any DRM which may be applied to this work.

# Table of Contents

About This Story ............................................................. 1
Content Notes ................................................................ 2
Dedication ...................................................................... 3
Chapter 1 ........................................................................ 4
Chapter 2 ........................................................................ 7
Chapter 3 ...................................................................... 12
Chapter 4 ...................................................................... 24
Chapter 5 ...................................................................... 26
Chapter 6 ...................................................................... 32
Chapter 7 ...................................................................... 36
Chapter 8 ...................................................................... 38
Chapter 9 ...................................................................... 41
Chapter 10 .................................................................... 45
Chapter 11 .................................................................... 55
Chapter 12 .................................................................... 58
Chapter 13 .................................................................... 62
Chapter 14 .................................................................... 65
Chapter 15 .................................................................... 71
Chapter 16 .................................................................... 74
Chapter 17 .................................................................... 77
Chapter 18 .................................................................... 79
Chapter 19 .................................................................... 83
Chapter 20 .................................................................... 85
Chapter 21 .................................................................... 87
Chapter 22 .................................................................... 94
Chapter 23 .................................................................... 96
Chapter 24 .................................................................. 101
Chapter 25 .................................................................. 108
Chapter 26 .................................................................. 112
Chapter 27 .................................................................. 115
Chapter 28 .................................................................. 116

Chapter 29 ............................................................................. 119
Chapter 30 ............................................................................. 120
Chapter 31 ............................................................................. 123
Chapter 32 ............................................................................. 126
Chapter 33 ............................................................................. 130
Chapter 34 ............................................................................. 133
Chapter 35 ............................................................................. 135
Chapter 36 ............................................................................. 138
Chapter 37 ............................................................................. 140
Chapter 38 ............................................................................. 142
Chapter 39 ............................................................................. 143
Chapter 40 ............................................................................. 147
Chapter 41 ............................................................................. 152
Chapter 42 ............................................................................. 159
Chapter 43 ............................................................................. 163
Chapter 44 ............................................................................. 168
Chapter 45 ............................................................................. 170
Chapter 46 ............................................................................. 175
Chapter 47 ............................................................................. 176
Chapter 48 ............................................................................. 183
Chapter 49 ............................................................................. 186
Chapter 50 ............................................................................. 189
Chapter 51 ............................................................................. 192
Chapter 52 ............................................................................. 196
Acknowledgements ............................................................. 200
Also by Tara Kennedy .......................................................... 202
About the Author ................................................................. 203
Troubled by Love Excerpt .................................................... 204

# About This Story

Lillian doesn't date bartenders. Xavier doesn't do secret relationships. They are both about to break their rules.

    Lillian's brother is a bartender, and the bartender circle in DC is too small for her to date within that pool. She meets a hot guy on the customer side of a bar and goes home with him. When she discovers he is a bartender too, she decides they never need to meet again. And that works, until he shows up to Thanksgiving dinner.

    Xavier's family drama means he likes things clear and upfront. But he never forgot Lillian, and when they end up seated at the same dinner table, he decides he'll agree to just about anything for another chance with her.

    Except secret relationships never stay secret for too long. When Lillian's brother and Xavier start looking into working together, Lillian and Xavier are either going to need to go public or end things.

# Content Notes

On page sex, reference to past parental/grandparental death, reference to past parental divorce, reference to COVID pandemic, reference to adoption discovery (secondary character), reference to pregnancy (secondary character).

# Dedication

To the newest T family member in my family, my sib-in-law. It seems fitting to dedicate a story about an older sister to you.

# Chapter 1

Lillian Yang enjoyed making and revising rules for herself almost as much as she liked trying out new concerts, and new bars and cocktails.

Once her brother became a bartender, finding a bar where no one knew her as Zane's sister became a challenge. But Lillian had never been on to let her younger brother spoil her fun. Not when they were kids. And certainly not now.

"Did you grow up around here?" she asked the bartender.

"Philly," the bartender said. "But my grandmother lives in Maryland, so we were down here a lot."

"What part of Maryland? I grew up in Silver Spring," Lillian said. She still lived there. Her brother had bought a condo in DC during a lucky spell in the real estate market. At the time, Lillian was dating her evil ex and had assumed they would buy something together.

Evil ex had turned out to be planning to borrow her identity. Wanted all her banking info for something other than mortgage pre-approval.

But no reason to let thoughts of him cloud the evening. She had set up a website, learned SEO, so that people who searched his name would find it. She had info about a lot of his past exes and the various financial and identity scams they had discovered he had involved them in.

And she set an alert. It had gone off again today. He was engaged again.

And Lillian decided to try out a new bar. Coincidentally.

"My grandmother is in Baltimore," the bartender said.

"Oh cool," Lillian said. "So, can I ask nosy questions about the owner?"

Lillian liked coming to bars for the first time on Tuesday. Things were a little more relaxed and she could find out quick if there were not enough degrees of separation between the bar staff and her brother.

"I actually don't know much about the owner. The hiring manager is cool though."

"The owner spends a lot of time in Connecticut," the guy two stools down said.

"Oh, is this place owned by Vance?" Lillian asked.

The bartender nodded. "Do you know him?"

"Of him," Lillian said, not sure if the question was for her or the dude on the stool, who was, she noticed, cute and quiet. Had only inserted himself in the conversation when he had something to offer. And hadn't immediately scooted over or tried to make his knowledge something the bartender or Lillian should care about.

"I've met him," dude said quietly. "I'm Xavier, by the way."

"Lillian."

"Della," the bartender said.

"Hey, Della," Xavier said pulling out some cash. "I gotta go, but you've been great as always. It was nice to meet you," he nodded at Lillian who nodded back. He walked out.

Lillian turned back. "Is he a regular?" He was cute, dark hair that waved enough to make her want to run her hands through it. If he was into that.

"Kind of," Della said. "But I should tell you, I've never seen him leave with anyone or take a number or anything. He comes in, orders one drink, and he leaves. Tips well, but that's it."

"Interesting." Lillian might have to hang out here more often. "So, outside of work do you do anything like knit? I'm always fascinated by people's hobbies."

"Knitting no, though my brother is big into crochet. He makes these little animals, it's cool. I read. When I'm not working, I don't need to move much. I can just curl up and read."

"Oh, have you read anything good lately? Also, you know about the bookstore just around the corner, right?"

"I do. I am a member and a regular there."

"Excellent. Well, if your brother - is he here or in Philly?"

"Good memory, he's in Philly."

"Well, if he comes down, I can show him the good yarn stores. And I'm finishing up a few audiobooks from the library right now, but when I need suggestions, I will definitely ask you."

"Planning on becoming a regular?"

"I think so. Am I allowed to call you Della, or is that weird?"

"You can. It's my name. And I love regulars. Want another drink to celebrate?"

"I believe I do," Lillian said.

# Chapter 2

Xavier Pika Strong unlocked the door to Bottom's Up and stood there breathing in the familiar scent of his bar. The smell of old alcohol lingered no matter how thoroughly they cleaned after closing.

He wished he could have stayed longer at Two Bars, but he liked to get here and take a look around before the staff arrived.

His phone buzzed. "Hi, Mom, I'm getting things ready for opening, is everything okay?"

"Hello to you to," his mom said. "Is that how you greet everyone? So rushed. What kind of customer service is that?"

"Are you a customer now?" Xavier knew he was playing with fire. But maybe he could deflect this, and turn this into a five-minute conversation, and not a two hour one. His mother worked as a financial planner. She had offered to help him invest the inheritance he had gotten from his grandmother, who had been mad enough at the rest of the family to leave all her cash to him.

Having fallen into bartending somewhat accidentally in college, he had discovered he like the rhythm of it.

His dad, a business consultant, had suggested Xavier use the money to get an MBA. Xavier had, somewhat immaturely been annoyed at both his parents after their messy divorce, so had instead bought a building where he could open a bar.

Xavier flicked on the lights in the back room and scanned the stock.

"I should be treated better than customers," Mom said.

"Okay, Mom."

His parents had both had suggestions for Xavier when the pandemic hit, about cutting his losses and getting a real job. Xavier's second place, a restaurant bar combo called Schism, had not survived. But Bottom's Up, rogue apostrophe and all, had managed to hang on. The drinks were bare bones, the decor was minimal, and the music was too. Their main clientele was people getting off restaurant shifts who wanted to drink somewhere that wasn't work.

"Okay, Mom," she repeated in a high-pitched voice. "So agreeable. Anyway, I wanted to know if you had gotten the retirement savings plan info that I sent to you. Even bartenders have to retire sometime you know. You won't be young forever."

"I did." Xavier said. The cider was low. He went and checked the stock room. It was tempting to leave the phone behind, but he carried it with him.

"And did you have any questions for me about anything? I can help you set things up."

"No questions, Mom." Xavier did not tell her he'd already talked to a financial advisor and set up an account for himself. He didn't talk to his mother about his finances any more.

She and his dad had spent months bickering over who should get this account or that account in the divorce. They had each called him trying to get him to take sides. "Well, he had a secret girlfriend, don't you think that means I should get more stock options." "Well, she had a secret girlfriend, don't you think that means I should get the retirement accounts. Her girlfriend is rich."

Xavier had hated it. Not so much that his parents were splitting, though that had been weird. Up until then he'd had no clue there were any issues in their relationship. But the spite over money, of all things, and then later over items, as they divvied up pieces of furniture. Fighting over who should get the couch, as if this couch they'd had for three years had some sentimental value.

Everything had been reduced to things, and they each seemed to want to win the divorce. And Xavier just wanted to have a discussion with either or both of his parents where he didn't have to pick a side. He wanted to talk about TV or sports, or even what Aunt Myrtle had decided to do with her hair.

But not things. Not money. And yet, his mother, these days, seemed to have decided he needed her help with money because the restaurant had closed.

"The restaurant business is so unstable. You have to make plans for your future."

Xavier nodded before remembering this was a phone call. "Got it."

Xavier loved his parents, but they made everything a tally. He hadn't selected the food and beverage industry because he liked working straight through November and December. But he could only imagine what ranks they would give the winter holidays if he spent one with either of them. His dad had gotten pissy one year because Xavier had given his mom a present for Mother's Day. Xavier had told his dad that he had a Father's Day gift for him, but Father's Day hadn't happened yet. His dad had then tried to write to his congressperson about setting up a rotation so that Father's Day happened first some years. But so far Congress was uninterested in solving this issue.

"Oh, another thing, Xavier," Mom said.

Xavier paused, sensing they were about to get to the real reason for the call. "Your cousin is talking about going on one of those TV shows, where they research your family. Isn't that ridiculous?"

"Which cousin?" Xavier asked. He placed the phone on the top of the case of cider and carried it into the bar. Checking the taps was next, but if he had to replace a keg, it was going to be noisy, so hopefully, the call would be over by then.

"Nani."

Nani was on the Hawaiian side of the family, Nani being Hawaiian for beautiful. Nani had grown up in Nevada, but had recently moved to New York because to become a model/actress/influencer. So, he figured being on TV was part of that plan.

"Cool," Xavier said. She had only moved to New York a few months ago, so that sounded like she was making things happen quickly.

"Your Auntie Nene is horrified. She wants Nani to back out. Uncle Alan is threatening to cut off her cell phone."

"Why?" Xavier asked, though he immediately regretted asking for more details. This was not how to slow down this conversation.

"I think Auntie Nene is worried that they'll dig up an unflattering picture or something. Plus, I bet she told her friends that Nani had gone off to college, and here she will be on TV, not in college."

Xavier rolled his eyes. A cell phone bill was much cheaper than college. Xavier didn't regret going, but college was super expensive. Costs had jumped even in the years since he had graduated. If she'd already figured out how to make a living without college, cool. And college would continue to exist. She could always go later if it made sense for her.

Parents needed to update how they bragged on their kids, in Xavier's opinion. No wait, actually, parents needed to stop judging their kids based on their ability to brag about them. Xavier smiled. He was sure if he told his mom that, it would go over just swell.

Or, she would tell him that someday, he would understand that you loved your kids so hard, that you worried about them, and wanted to tell other people about how they were doing. Xavier wasn't quite sure how being born, being loved, should mean everything reflected back all the time. But that was not a conversation he expected to win today, or honestly ever.

"Xavier, are you still there?" his mom asked.

"Right here, Mom," he said. "But I do have to finish getting everything ready. Was that everything you wanted to tell me?"

"Yes. Well, and you should check on your father."

"Any special reason?" Xavier asked.

"I'll let him explain," his mom said cryptically. "Okay, I gotta go sweetie, bye."

"Bye, Mom," Xavier said.

Xavier had five more minutes before Mateo and Bailey would show up. He looked around. The glasses and kegs all looked good. He dialed his dad's number but it went to voicemail. His dad's voicemail was a black hole. Xavier texted his dad.

Xavier: How's everything going?

Vague, but better than, Mom said you have something to tell me.

No answer. Xavier pocketed his phone and went to open the back door for Mateo.

# Chapter 3

"Lillian, we've got a donor coming in who wants to eat somewhere fun. Any suggestions?" her boss Georgia asked.

"Does it matter what kind of food?" Lillian had kind of accidentally become the person in the office people asked about this stuff, even though it wasn't her job. But she enjoyed tracking all the goings on in the city, so she didn't mind,

"Well, he's flying in from China so probably not Asian," Georgia said.

"There is a Peruvian Chinese fusion place. It might be sort of the same but different. There's also a Portuguese tapas place."

"Can you send me both of those? I'll let him decide."

"Sure." Lillian nodded.

By the time Lillian left work, she was ravenous. There was no food in her apartment so, she stopped at the grocery store. She picked up a super easy meal kit, even though her brain was whispering, screw all this, let's get tacos. But no, she was being responsible.

But once home, super easy meal kit turned out to be a big fat lie. Somehow the pasta was sticky, and the sauce thin, and why was making food just annoying like that sometimes? Lillian hod not picked up any frozen meals at the store. She checked her freezer, nope, nothing lingering in there waiting to be eaten. This new leaf she was turning over where she was going to try to cooking more and eating prepared stuff less sucked.

Screw it. She was going to go get tacos. And in the taco place was near Two Bars, the bar she had enjoyed last week, well, it would just be neighborly to stop in. Lillian pulled up her contacts wondering if she should text anyone to join her. For some reason, she wanted to go solo tonight.

It wasn't anything like hoping that guy would be there again and trying to keep him to herself, because that would be presumptuous and rude.

But Lillian did check her lipstick, and head out to the taco place. The weather was still warm enough to eat outside, even if the leaves were already turning. Lillian enjoyed the people watching when sitting at the street-side tables. A couple walked by with a dog that had that fluffy curly fur. See, who needed to cook, when eating out provided so much entertainment.

Lillian ignored the voice that mentioned eating out was expensive and cooking was an important life skill. Lillian could cook. But she wasn't skilled at making new things without stumbles, and probably that was a thing that would improve with more practice, but the learning curve sucked.

She walked over to the bar, and peeked inside. Della was there but it was Wednesday and things looked otherwise empty. "Hey there, Della," Lillian said taking a seat. "Read anything good lately?"

"Hello, it was Lillian, right?" Della asked.

"Good memory," Lillian said.

Della brought her a drink. "I've been on a fantasy kick lately."

"Oh cool. Titles please." Lillian pulled out her phone and stared making notes. The phone buzzed in her hand. It was a call from her mom. Her mom usually didn't call this late. "Hey, Mom, everything okay?"

"Yes, yes," her mom said. "What was the name of the place we ordered food from last year?"

Lillian mouthed "sorry" at Della. "Ordered takeout or something else?" Lillian was trying to actually think if they had ordered takeout last year. Zane and Lillian were always trying to get their mom to let them bring dinner over or something, Louise too now. But usually, she told them to save their money.

"For Thursday," her mom said.

"For this Thursday?" Lillian was completely confused.

"For the Fourth Thursday," her mom said.

Oh. Lillian remembered her mom had told her that the ladies at her church had decided that Thanksgiving was regressive, but also gathering with family and eating seasonal food was good. So apparently, they were calling it Fourth Thursday now. Which sure. "Last year I think we ordered from Zane's friend's place."

"Okay, can you ask your brother to order again? And remember we'll need enough for Louise too."

"Got it," Lillian said. She wasn't really in danger of forgetting Louise existed, nor was Zane. Louise was part of the family. Louise's parents traveled a lot, and weren't into celebrating holidays as a family which simplified the whose family will we hang out with for the holidays stuff. Or it seemed like it did to Lillian.

She also wasn't sure why she was calling Zane, instead of her mom, but it wasn't exactly a hardship.

"Thanks, bye," Mom said, hanging up quickly.

Lillian shook her head. She texted Zane.

Lillian: Hey, Mom wants to order for Thanksgiving/Fourth Thursday from the same place as last year. I can do it, just need the name.

Zane: I'll do it. Same food and all, any changes? I'll check their menu, but I think they were pretty much offering all the same stuff.

Lillian: I can pick it up too. I know your schedule is tricky to plan out.

Zane had gone back to picking up shifts at Circle Bar after he had to close the restaurant he had been managing. But they didn't have a whole empty shift for him, so he had been doing a lot of filling in and covering for others. The afternoon bartender had another job starting soon, but it had gotten delayed and so, things were just a lot. Well, according to Zane they were all just fine. Lillian only knew most of this, because Louise had told her.

Zane: We'll see what pick up slot they give us. Also Louise said to tell you she loves the cowel? sp?

Lillian: Cowl. And yay.

Zane: We made tons of chili, btw. You should come raid the fridge.

The door to the bar swung open and the guy Lillian had been hoping to see wandered in.

\*\*\*

Xavier liked to stop in at various bars throughout the city to get a feel for the vibe each was crafting. Owning a bar was more than a full-time job, but these short stop ins were useful. It helped remind him what it was like to be on the other side. It also was nice to be in a bar and not be in charge of anything.

And okay, he kept an eye on great bartenders. Mateo and Bailey had been with him forever. Dan had worked for him for a bunch of years, but recently was focusing more on his soup business.

Xavier had offered Zane a job, another job when their restaurant had closed. But Zane had gone back to Circle, citing that he liked the hours better.

Xavier wondered if there was more to it. He wouldn't blame Zane managing a restaurant amid and pandemic, and then ultimately closing that restaurant had soured Zane on working with Xavier.

He'd watched plenty of people, change things up, so they could at least pretend the pandemic stress must surely have been left behind with that old job, old partner, old city even.

But tonight, Bottom's Up was fully staffed. Bailey had taken his keys and told him he could stop by once to check on them, but he needed to be at least an hour after they opened. And that they would text if anything they couldn't handle came up.

There was a new speakeasy type deal he wanted to check out, but he had walked down from his apartment and spotted the sign for Two Bars and just thought, there. He could stop in, order a drink, and then by the time he got to Bottom's Up, it would be close enough to the time Bailey had said.

Xavier didn't always let his employees get their way. But he had been encouraging all of them to take their days off. So, it was hard to push back when they insisted he do the same.

He waved to Della as he walked in and gave her an order as he sat down.

That woman was back too. He had noticed her because he always checked out the customers in bars where the bartender was staffed alone. Vance staffed that way on low turnover days in a lot of his bars, and Xavier was not a fan. He got why, paying two to three people minimum wage on days that had few customers got expensive quickly. But so did the one employee you had staffed getting sick, or having an issue with a customer that made them feel unsafe, or they just plain lost their keys to the bar. Also, if you only had one employee staffed, how did they use the bathroom? There were just way too many issues.

And so, when he was in somewhere that did that, he kept an eye on the customers. Okay, once he had learned to scope out customers, he found he did it everywhere. But also, she had gorgeous dark hair, was kind, and talked to Della like she was a person, not a customer service bot. It was increasingly unusual behavior these days.

He listened to her and Della talk books. He used to love reading, but bar owner life meant he listened to a lot of people, and in his leisure time, or while he was doing paperwork, he ended up listening to music. But he should try getting back into that. He pulled out his phone and made a quick note of some of the titles they mentioned.

"One more?" Della asked him. Xavier shouldn't but he was enjoying himself, so why not. "Okay," he said.

"Aw crud, I need to change it out. Can I trust you two alone out here for a bit? You can yell if anyone else comes in."

"We got you," the woman said.

Xavier nodded.

Della gave them a thumbs up and walked dragged the empty keg into the back.

"Those things look so heavy, even when they are empty," the woman said. Lillian, that was her name.

"It's not too bad when they are empty." Xavier was also used to lugging them around full, but he used a cart, because he wanted his employees to use a cart. Only have to watch one person's toe turn ridiculous colors after they drop it, to want to make that a policy. Hopefully, Della had a cart back there. But no, Xavier was not in charge here. And Della knew what she was doing.

"You look like you want to add something."

"No, I'm just reminding myself that I'm not working here," Xavier said. He reached for his glass to give himself something to do before he remembered that it was empty.

"Is reminding yourself you are not at work something you have to do a lot of?"

"Well, I usually am at work or am doing something related to work, so possibly," Xavier said. Oh wow, he had not really thought about how true that was. He didn't aspire to be Vance, but there was something to having figured out how to own places that you just checked in on once a while. He used to have a hobby. Probably.

"Ah, well, the good news is that there is a lot of that going around in this city, and there are solutions. Did you want solutions, or am I ruining your woe is me moment?"

Xavier laughed. "You can move past my woe is me moment. What are your solution proposals?"

"I'm a big fan of crafts. Knitting. Or leisure stuff like reading. But maybe you're more of a concerts and hiking kind of guy."

"Concerts are not a bad idea. I tend to work weekends though."

"Oh, there's tons of live music venues in this area. Plenty of them have weekday gigs. Are you new in town?"

Xavier laughed. "No, I grew up here. But the last time I was at a concert was probably," he tried to think back, "I think the stadium had a different name, so I could use a refresher."

"Well, and in the summer there's a lot of outdoor events, though most of those have wrapped for the season. And a lot of those are free which is nice,"

"You're very knowledgeable about all of this. Are you a social planner?"

"Officially, I am in strategic communications, but unofficially, my boss does seem to think I am a social planner, so I do keep track of a lot of events."

"Is that normal for your boss to also want you to be a social planner?"

"I did this to myself. See, like right after I got hired, when I was still new and eager, she said something to the effect of, I wish I knew where to take these folks for dinner. And I rattled off like two suggestions. And then, she kept asking me, and I started tracking new restaurants and various other things. I mean, I make it sound hard. I basically signed up for a bunch of newsletters, and read the local coverage of stuff, and I summarize things. It's not that hard, but she now gets the other execs to ask me too."

Xavier looked over and wondered if Della was okay. Of course, maybe she was taking a break. Another thing that was hard to do when you were staffed alone. Xavier wasn't in a hurry. He was enjoying listening to how Lillian thought.

"Maybe you should create your own newsletter and subscribe them all to it," Xavier said.

"I thought about it. But I think they like imagining that they are tapping into my young hip knowledge. I'm Lillian by the way. Did we cover that before?"

"I'm Xavier. And we did, but no worries. I live not too far from here, so while I do try to keep tabs on bars in the city, this place is close by." Bottom's Up was also close by. He had managed to score a place close to work, after he bought the bar. Useful when the weather sucked, and if anyone called out last minute. But it did mean he had to make an effort to go other places to drink.

"I'm in Silver Spring, so not too far."

Xavier nodded. "They have good bars in Silver Spring too. Not that I'm against people traveling. Especially if you have to keep track of all the goings on in the city."

"Well, I don't give them all the good stuff. Some of the cool bars and other info I hang on to for myself. Can't be letting the good places get overrun by execs and their clients."

"Ah, there's a lot that goes into this, I see."

"So," Lillian said. "Obviously, we would wait for Della to return and settle up and all of that. But how interested are you in showing me exactly how close by your place is?"

Xavier was very, very interested.

\* \* \*

Lillian had once met someone who claimed to live nearby, and then started typing an address a county and a half away into the rideshare app. She had decided, despite his cuteness, that she did not want to learn what a rideshare that far away costs, and had instead ordered her own rideshare home. Also, while not every hookup required much more common ground than, you cute, let's do it, anyone who thought a county and a half away counted as close, was not to be trusted. Who knows what else they might consider close. Might be okay leaving her with half an orgasm, and while Lillian certainly knew how to fix that, she did not need to road trip to do it.

Della came back apologizing that she had taken so long. Xavier and Lillian both waved that off, and put cash on the bar. "I'll be back after I read that book, if not sooner," Lillian said as she and Xavier walked outside.

"I live right there," Xavier said pointing to a building across the street.

"Oh, so when you said close, you meant close." Lillian shivered a little. A person who meant close had to be a good sign right? Maybe she should have kissed him first. But she also knew how to leave and get home easily enough. So she wasn't worried. Though she texted her knitting friend the info. Torrey texted a thumbs up emoji back.

They made their way across the street and up the stairs and into a surprisingly neat apartment. There was a small desk surrounded by organized files in the living room, the couch and TV were both spacious, and there was no trail of laundry or well, scattered crafts about. Lillian supposed that was one advantage of being a workaholic. The kitchen area looked clean but not unused.

If his bed had an actual headboard, he'd be way ahead of her in the adulting games.

Xavier toed off his shoes and left them on a small mat by the door. Lillian did the same.

"I know we just left a bar, but do you need a drink or anything?" Xavier asked.

Lillian smiled. "How about a kiss?"

"Oh yeah, I guess, we just skipped over that."

She leaned in and kissed him. The time for words, well, not all the words, but many of them was done now. His lips were soft and he tasted a little of alcohol, and as she shifted closer, her body heated and she felt the faint buzz of excitement coursing through her. This was just what she needed, wanted.

Lillian loved the anticipation. This moment where the kiss was filled with the promise of what was next.

"My bedroom is that way. Or we could stay here. Whichever," Xavier said.

Lillian smiled. "Condoms?" She usually carried some in her purse, but had changed purses today and wasn't sure the condoms had made it in. Mental note to fix that later.

"I have some." Xavier turned and went down the short hallway. She followed peeking into the bedroom. Also clean, bed made even. And yep, he had a headboard. It was metal and looked old.

He held out a box of condoms and she grabbed a few, checking the expiration dates. "Cool." She tossed them on the bed and started stripping her clothes off. Xavier stripped down and Lillian climbed onto the bed, pausing a moment to admire the shape of his body. He gestured her closer to the edge of the bed putting gentle hands on her knees.

"This good?" he asked.

Lillian nodded. His hand slid down her thigh, spreading her wide, gently stroking over her clit. She pushed her hand over his pressing harder. He took over leaning down to swipe his tongue over her, nudging her to tilt her hips to give him more access. She moaned as he slid a finger inside her, stroking her inside as he continued to suck her clit. She felt the orgasm building inside her, and then it broke over her,

Xavier pulled his finger out of her, and then slid the condom on while Lillian was still trying to see straight.

He moved onto the bed and propped himself on his side, seemingly in no rush, despite the condom. Lillian shifted herself so she mirrored his position and then reached out and ran a hand across his chest, feeling the smooth skin. Her hand slid over his high and then across his thigh. She shifted closer, leaving very little space between them. She moved her hand back, cupping his buttock. Despite having just came she was excited to do more, but also having trouble deciding on a plan of approach, though she enjoyed the chance to think about it. Xavier seemed in no hurry.

She shifted a little closer, and moved one leg, hooking it across him, bringing them even closer together. He shifted again and kissed her.

Oh, his kisses were good. She tugged him a little closer with her leg. He grasped her waist and shifted them so he was above her and then asked, "Ready?"

"Yes," Lillian breathed. They moved together, him inside her. They shifted finding a rhythm, and she spread her legs wider, and he sped up his movements, and she could feel it building again, more. He reached between them and stroked her clit hard and she came. And a few thrusts later felt him shudder in completion.

They lay there, sweat cooling. He reached down and slowly pulled out, getting up to dispose of the condom.

Lillian sat up. There was always that moment after good sex where she had so much energy, but she knew she'd crash in like ten minutes, and she should get home, because tomorrow was a workday.

Xavier came back in, still naked.

Or she could stay.

"You could stay," Xavier said. "I don't have to work until late tomorrow."

"What's late for you?" Lillian asked, twining her hair. Twisting and twining her hair helped her think.

"Like 5."

"5 a.m. is not late." Lillian stood and started gathering her clothes.

"p.m.," Xavier said.

"5 p.m.?" Lillian said. "The only kind of..." she trailed off. The jobs that started at 5 p.m. could be many things. Hotel staff, hospital, maintenance, theater crew. It could also be bartender.

"I own a bar. I like checking out other bars in the area, so sometimes I stop in at Two Bars," Xavier said.

"Oh cool," Lillian said with what she hoped was a believable smile as she started putting all her clothes on. "I have to work a little earlier than that, and I wouldn't want you to have to wake up early just for me, so I should probably go. But this was great." Lillian kept smiling. All those people who said smiling took less muscles than other expressions were clearly big fat liars who could not be trusted. She could feel her face muscles straining. But this was fine. She was just going to leave.

"I can walk you out. And maybe we could do this again sometime?"

"Yeah, maybe," Lillian said. She tapped the rideshare app up, and prayed for quick and speedy service. Three minutes away. Okay. She could make it through three minutes.

She walked back into the living room and did a quick scan to make sure she hadn't forgotten anything.

Xavier had gotten dressed. They slid on their shoes and walked down to the stoop. She looked, and yes, the car, was pulling right up. The advantage of hooking up with people who lived near bars. Of course, maybe she should have considered that she was close to where her brother lived. But surely not everyone who lived around here worked in a bar. But yes, useful screening question going. forward.

"Lillian?" the driver asked.

"Yep, that's me." She slid in and waved. The driver pulled away quickly, probably because there was another car behind them, but she was grateful. And she was going to focus on how nice it was being able to make a quick getaway after good sex. And worry about the can never see that guy again and also that meant Two Bars was off the list too. Bummer.

She had liked that bar. She had liked Xavier too. But boundaries were important. And well, he got a good time too tonight. There just wouldn't be any repeats.

# Chapter 4

"So, Xavier," Bailey said. "I'm pregnant."

"Oh, Bailey, how great!" Xavier got up from where he'd been working on the schedule at the end of the bar, and came around to hug her. Bailey and her partner Tomas had been working on that for a bit.

"Thanks," Bailey said. "I'm going to need to be taking time for appointments and stuff. Because of my history, I'm high risk, so it will be kind of a lot. I have a friend I think can pitch in to cover some of my shifts if you want me to give her a call."

"Yeah, okay. I'll reach out to some folks too. But just let me know the days you need, and we'll figure all of that out."

"Okay."

"Oh and, you can tell everyone I said you weren't allowed to lift things."

"They really only worry about that in first trimester, but yeah. I'll use the lift."

"You should always use the lift."

"Yes, boss, of course. That's what I meant."

Well, now Xavier was going to have stress dreams about that. So that was fun.

But none of that would solve this scheduling issue. Xavier sat back in front of his computer and stared at the spreadsheet.

The spreadsheet was more likely to have a solution than his Lillian problem. Xavier hadn't gotten Lillian's number. There were a couple of possibilities. It could be intentional. She could have been after a hookup and nothing more. He wasn't against hookups. He just had enjoyed talking to her, and yes, also enjoyed having sex with her, and he wanted to do more of both. Lillian knew where he lived, but he wouldn't blame her if knocking on someone's door and being like, so, should we hang out more just seemed awkward. He had googled Lillian Silver Spring, there were enough of them that he wasn't able to narrow it down further. Even the social media accounts had been more than he was willing to peruse. Besides she might be Lilli or Lily or some other variation on her social media. Lots of people did plays on their name.

He had stopped in at Two Bars a few times. Della hadn't seen her either. So. Lillian had enough information to get back in contact with him. And he didn't. So, he just had to hope she would. He knew this many weeks later, the odds were not good. DC was just big enough that you didn't constantly run into people you know. But with the transplant churn, it often brought you back into contact with folks who stayed a lot. He was constantly running into folks he went to school with, or who turned out to be the kid of his third-grade teacher, or some other little connection. So, he'd see her again. And maybe she'd be interested in a repeat.

Xavier focused on the schedule. He needed another employee, but the budget wasn't going to stretch to an entire person just yet. If someone like Dan or Zane would reliably pick up some extra shifts, that would work better. Xavier sent off a text to each of them. He could also put an ad up somewhere. So many of his employees had been referrals or had just shown up and asked if he needed anyone. Well, he could at least post something on the website. Almost no one looked at that, but it would make him feel like he had done something.

Bailey had said she had a friend who might be able to cover, so that might work too. Or maybe he could steal Della.

Not steal. She was a person after all. But borrow. Encourage to leave a steady job where she got all the tips for one where they did tip sharing? Maybe she'd be into that. It certainly wouldn't hurt to ask. It was nice to have a plan of sorts.

# Chapter 5

"I wish there was more of a music scene here. I miss going to concerts," said Isabel.

Lillian looked up from her knitting. Isabel had mentioned that she had just moved to DC, so Lillian was willing to give her like a tiny bit of grace for being wrong. "There's actually a thriving music scene here. What are you looking for - stadium sized stuff, smaller venues, grunge, punk, pop, folk?"

Torrey smiled at Lillian. "Lillian is always keeping track of all the cool goings on in the area."

"Not all of them," Lillian said. "I like to sleep too. But yeah, I keep an eye out. And of course, there's some good local news sources that it helps if you sign up for."

"Oh gosh," Isabel said. "I signed up for one thing that lots of people recommended, but I ended up getting so much spam about bathrobes and facials, that I unsubscribed from everything. But yeah, I like a variety of music, but smaller venues where like a night won't cost an entire paycheck is my jam."

"I get that. Give me your info, I'll send you some ideas and you can take a look."

"I remember, back in the day Susan and I used to go to concerts like once a week it felt like," Emilia said.

"I know," Alex said, "now I can't even imagine standing much less dancing for that long.

"You all are not that old. Isabel's going to think we're all decrepit the way you talk," Regan said.

"When was the last time you went to a concert?" Alex said.

"This summer, Bobby and I went to one at the Birchmere."

"Oh, the Birchmere has seats. That doesn't count."

"Lots of places that have concerts have seats. Are you telling me there aren't seats at the Beyonce concert?"

"Did you go to the Beyonce concert?"

"No, I got stuck on the waitlist. But I watched clips. It looked amazing."

"My daughter and I went," Emilia said. "It was amazing."

Lillian grabbed Isabel's contact information. She already had a few ideas, but she'd text her later. It was fun connecting others with fun.

"Hey, what ever happened with that guy?" Torrey asked. "The one you texted me about."

Lillian gave Torrey a death glare. Some of the knitting crew were very happily coupled up. And of course, they thought that meant that Lillian should also be happily coupled up. Not even the story of the identity stealing ex had deterred them for longer than a minute. Lillian usually saved talk about her sex life for when it was just her and Torrey. Because let someone hold a door open for her, and they were all on her, like you should talk to them, find out if they're single.

It was very sweet, but also Lillian really liked being single, being able to do her own thing and not check in with others. Louise and Zane were very cute together, and Zane's friends all seem to be coupling up at a rapid rate. Lillian had been a bridesmaid six times right after college, had been sure she's be calling all those folks to be her bridesmaid with the ex. And then it hadn't happened and life had gone on. She'd dated others, slept with quite a few. And some of those folks she'd worn pastel for, weren't with their spouses anymore. Relationships worked until they didn't and Lillian wasn't against finding someone she wanted to do more than hookup with. But she also didn't want to spend so much time focused on finding the one, that she missed all the delicious stops she could make along the way.

"It was fun, but not my type for the long run," she said. A tiny part of her felt bad for that lie. It was true that she had a no bartender rule. She had hooked up a few times with Kayne after the ex. Kayne was tall, blonde, and bartending while he worked on his next great idea. The kind of guy who told people, including Lillian, that he loved bartending because he got free alcohol and first pick of the hotties. Lillian had had no concerns that they were exclusive or that, barring one or both of them having a huge life change, that they had anything resembling a future. But he had been good in bed, and sometimes a person who flirts with everyone was just the thing she wanted.

But Zane had apparently been feeling overprotective and had gotten wind of it. And instead of Zane checking with her, or maybe just minding his own business, he had decided to tell Kayne that Lillian was vulnerable and did not deserve to be treated as a hookup. And Kayne, instead of telling Zane to fuck off, or asking Lillian what she wanted, had told her maybe they should back off because she seemed to need something more.

Lillian had then told Zane to butt out. He had apologized but in that way that told her he was apologizing because he was supposed to, not because he understood why. And so, it was simpler to just not to sleep with bartenders. In the interest of family harmony. Or it had been, until she forgot and hooked up with a hot guy who turned out to be a bartender. He had been cute, and fun to talk with, and she wondered if he had read one of the books she suggested.

She had tried asking at the bookstore about Della, but she hadn't gone back to Two Bars. If Xavier was a bartender, she could be fairly certain he wouldn't show up on a Friday or Saturday night. But he lived so close, even going to the nearby bookstore had felt like a covert operation.

"You know, I was so sure I knew my type," Eileen said. "And then I met my Teddy."

Lillian smiled and nodded, because yes, she had heard this all before. And Teddy was lovely. And Lillian was very happy for them. Lillian glanced over at Torrey again who did not look even a little bit sorry. Lillian looked closer. What had they been talking about before? Had Torrey been trying to change the subject. Lillian pulled out her phone.

Lillian: You are super dead. But you doing okay?

Torrey pulled out her phone and stared at it for longer than Lillian would have expected for such a simple question. Torrey glanced up and saw Lillian looking at her and texted back a thumbs up emoji.

Um okay. Lillian had never been so sure an emoji was a lie in her life. Torrey lived with her partner Arielle. Maybe something had happened there, and that was why they were all now sharing their how I met the love of my life stories.

One thing Lillian had learned was not everything was repeatable. It was human nature to try and mimic other people's successes. If you wanted cake, you followed the recipe exactly and you got cake. In theory. Lillian had certainly had some mishaps even when she was following the recipe.

Similarly, she had met people to date and hook up with in person, by going to bars, and also on the apps, or through friends. But telling someone else, I met a cute guy by going to this bar on a Tuesday wasn't necessarily a repeatable data point. Louise had gone one a date with a guy who turned out to have lined up several dates for the exact same evening. It was a terrible idea, even if Lillian understood the impulse. Having never met the guy, her best guess is he was trying to do a controlled experiment. Bad food or bad service could color your entire experience about a night. Setting all the dates on the same night in the same bar, made that part as similar as possible. Of course, treating the people you were dating like experimental subjects was not a route to finding someone because people weren't subjects.

But Lillian wasn't in a relationship primarily because she didn't want to be. Not because she was too picky. Too picky about the people you dedicate your time to shouldn't even be a thing. Maybe if she dumped him for his condiment preferences. But even then. Who wanted to spend the rest of their life arguing over what condiments went on the fries?

Lillian walked out with Torrey as they wrapped up their evening. "So for real, you doing okay?"

"Yeah," Torrey said. "Arielle and I just had a fight and like, it's fine, but also," Torrey sighed.

"I'm sorry," Lillian said.

"So what type was that guy that he was the wrong type?"

"He was a bartender, well, bar owner, I guess. Same deal," Lillian said.

"You didn't ask beforehand? He must have been cute."

"He was. He also said he was a workaholic and well, I assumed he had some paper pushing job that I didn't really want to hear about. But yes, will vet better in the future."

They swiped their metro cards and got down to the platform to wait for the train. "So, do you want to talk about the fight?" Lillian asked.

"Oh, it was one of those things. She asked if I was going to knitting tonight, and I was like of course. And then she was like we never do anything together, and I was like we hang out all the time. And she was like, but we never go out, and I pointed out she's always talking about how she needs to save money for the family wedding she's got to go to in a few months, and so on. She was still mad when she left for her in office day, so like we haven't had a chance to talk about it. It's probably fine."

Lillian waited as the train pulled in and they managed to find two seats together. Torrey lived downtown, so got off sooner than Lillian. "Do you want suggestions or just to vent?"

"Suggestions for not fighting?"

"Oh no, I have no suggestions for that. I meant like suggestions for cheap things y'all can do?"

"Y'all? Aren't you from Maryland?"

"We say y'all in Maryland."

"Okay, we all, w'all, whatever, I mean, maybe? I do think she's just bored. Like obviously she could come to knitting, but she doesn't want to knit, and if we all spend twenty minutes talking about patterns and swatches, that part isn't interesting."

"How often do we spend time talking about patterns and swatches?" Lillian asked. "Never mind. Like I get it. She doesn't want to come and just feel like the plus one. But there are - well less free concerts and movies now that it's fall, but there are things that are like cheap to low cost. The library does lots of events."

"About books?"

"I'm going to pretend I didn't hear you say that like it wasn't the most exciting thing ever. Yes, many of their events are about books. They also do concerts. There's also the Zoo. And like eighty million museums."

"Eighty million?"

"That figure might be slightly exaggerated. But the Botanical Gardens, one of the parks, you could basically buy bread and cheese and meat and picnic like four thousand places."

"Four thousand? Do you do this at work? Should I assume your work newsletter is filled with exaggerated figures?"

"No, we have footnotes to all our sources in the work newsletter."

"Fine. Send us some suggestions. No wait, send them to me, and I will take credit for them."

"That's fine," Lillian said. She already had a few ideas. "Also, I have an air mattress if you want to really not go home."

"It will be fine. But I appreciate the offer." Torrey waved as she got up for her stop.

Lillian sent a text to herself to remind her to send concert info to Isabel and cheap date ideas to Torrey. Being a fun planner was fun. This should be a real job.

# Chapter 6

"I appreciate you coming in on short notice," Xavier said to Zane. Bailey had called out. Matteo was going to come in later, but he and Dan were both in a health code training course of some sort. Normally Xavier would just cover things by himself, but he needed to make an alcohol order and they had either misplaced or mismarked three cases of beer. Xavier wanted to sort through the inventory and figure out which it was.

"It's fine," Zane said. "Louise might stop by, but she's got some big project at work. So, we will see."

Xavier nodded.

Xavier's phone rang the second the door swung shut behind him. So much for organizing the inventory. He's been trying to reach his dad for more than a hey, how's it going for a few weeks, so sending him to voicemail when he called seemed rude. Tempting but rude.

"Hi, Dad," Xavier said.

"What are we doing for Thanksgiving?" Xavier's father asked.

Xavier had pre-ordered some food from a local restaurant for Thanksgiving. He could cook, but the week of Thanksgiving was the busiest week at the bar, and so he spent even more time that usual on his feet. So, he let other people cook. But he didn't think his father meant where did you order from. But he and his father didn't talk on the phone much, so maybe he did mean that.

"I'm gonna eat early and then I'll be at the bar."

"Aren't you the owner?" Dad said.

Xavier had always been the owner. It was close to a decade now. Which his dad knew. "Yes, dad," he said trying not to sound like a petulant teenager.

"Shouldn't the owner have staff to work holidays?"

Ah yes. That's what his father meant. "I have staff, and I also help out on what is literally our busiest week of the year." Xavier had made a chart once, a very pretty chart if he said so himself, of Thanksgiving sales, and New Years, and Christmas sales, at the bar. He had briefly wondered if a pitch deck might get through to his parents when the words had not. But then he decided that they'd just find something else to nag about, so he had not sent it to them.

His parents were smart people. And he understood that people liked gathering with loved ones in the darker days of the year, and when the work lightened up for a bit. The first year his parents were split, they were both still in DC. They had divided the townhouse into pieces and created a schedule for things like the kitchen. Xavier had come home for Thanksgiving and they had explained this to him with his mother standing in the kitchen and his dad standing in the adjacent living room. His dad had asked if he could bring him a snack from the fridge, and his mom had snapped that he wasn't to use Xavier as a gopher to get around the schedule. Of course, an hour later, she asked him to bring her a slice of pie.

Xavier had escaped. Gone for a walk, and ended up in a bar. He wasn't twenty-one yet, but the bartender handed him a glass of water and didn't hassle him about taking up a stool even though the place got packed quickly.

When he had turned twenty-one, that bar had hired him on for the summer.

As for breaks, Xavier had stayed on campus as much as possible after that. Now, with his dad in North Carolina and his mom in New York, even if it wasn't his businesses busiest time of year, he'd probably stay in DC. It avoided letting holiday stays get added to the points total in his parents' war.

"So you'll be in DC?" Dad asked.

"Yes, I will," Xavier said. One year he had suggested that March would be a great time to gather. That he could visit each of his parents, or they could visit him. But they had ignored it, then fought over which parent he should visit first, sending competing travel plans. Xavier had finally booked a hotel in Atlantic City, sent them the info and the dates and told them they could come join him. Neither of them did.

"I don't think I'm up for travel at the moment. You may have heard that Julie and I broke up," Dad said. "Is your mom going to be in DC?"

"Not as far as I know," Xavier said. "And I'm sorry about Julie." Xavier guessed that was the thing his mom had been hinting at. He wasn't even going to wonder how she knew.

"Well, if you do decide to come to North Carolina, let me know."

"Will do," Xavier said.

An hour later his phone rang again. Xavier placed the laptop safely on top of the stack of cans he was loading into the back fridge,

"Hi, Mom," Xavier said.

"What are we doing for Thanksgiving?" she asked.

"I will be working," Xavier said. "Busiest day of the year and all."

"Really, working again?" Mom said.

Xavier's mom was a workaholic herself, so he could never quite figure out what she meant by working again. When was it that he was meant to have stopped? She had once had her assistant come down to the hospital with her, when she had was turned out to be a burst appendix. Because she said there was no point in wasting time while waiting in the ER, and it wasn't like her appendix was even a crucial organ.

"Well, your cousin is cooking the whole dinner for your aunt and uncle. Won't let them lift a finger even."

Xavier had thought his cousin had moved away, but maybe they were talking about a different cousin now. There were a lot of cousins.

"How nice."

"Isn't it? I supposed I'll need to have my assistant figure out what catering options there are."

Xavier refrained from saying that she should do that soon. The place he ordered his own dinner from had sold out last week. But his mom was probably going to order from a larger chain, not a small business. And well, that was her assistant's problem, not his.

"What's your father doing for Thanksgiving?"

"Staying home," Xavier said.

"Well, I hope he knows you have to think about food in advance."

Xavier made a non-committal sound.

"Well, we should talk soon. I have to go. Bye,"

"Bye." Xavier wondered if his dad did know that you needed to pre-order food on Thanksgiving. He could text him. But despite what his mom thought, his dad really was an adult who did know how take care of himself, even if he was often surprised at the things that doing so required.

Xavier: Dad, make sure you've got food ordered for Thanksgiving.

His dad didn't text back. But he was sure his dad would eventually see it. Or it would be Thursday and his dad would forget and just eat regular food.

Not everyone had to eat turkey to be happy on Thanksgiving.

# Chapter 7

"Lillian, did you order food?" her mom asked.

"Yes, well, Zane did because he's friends with the manager there."

"Did you check the order? Sometimes your brother gets distracted. Though maybe he had Louise look at it. She's very detail oriented."

"Yes, it got checked," Lillian said vaguely. Zane was entirely competent at making food orders.

"And all of you are coming here?"

"Yes, Mom. Anything we can bring besides the food?"

"No just food and you guys, that's all I need. Well, and napkins. But I have those. I will do lots of laundry."

"Yep. I'll be there." Lillian opened a new tab on her web browser and looked to see if she could get a plant to bring to her mom.

"So, it's just four, right?" her mom asked.

"Four people?" Lillian asked making sure she knew what they were talking about. It could be four pies after all. Hmm, she opened another tab. Maybe another pie. Or two. Or four.

"Yes, for dinner."

"You, me, Louise, and Zane. That's four." Lemon pie sounded delicious. She added on to her cart.

"So, no one else is coming?"

"Not that I'm aware of. Are you bringing someone else, Mom?"

"Me, who would I bring? I meant you. Are you bringing someone?"

Ah. Lillian flipped back to the plants tab. Maybe a cactus. She had sort of known that once Louise and Zane became a thing, she was on borrowed time. She was the oldest and a girl, so of course she was supposed to crave coupledom and all the accompanying accoutrements. She wasn't even against coupledom, she just wasn't going to go grab someone just because somebody had decided she was supposed to. This wasn't musical chairs. She wasn't going to lose her chance.

"No, I am not bringing anyone to Thanksgiving, Mom." Also, Lillian would hardly have invited someone and not told her mom. That was the kind of thing that Zane would do. Well, not now. Because Louise would tell them.

"You should think about it. Louise was meeting people for appetizers."

Louise was - oh she meant apps. Lousie had been meeting dates on an app. Louise had also not met Zane on an app. Though, Lillian supposed Louise had met Zane because he worked in the bar she met her dates at. So technically the apps had brought them together. Even if Zane had never once, as far as Lillian knew, been on a dating app. Though she didn't tell Zane about any apps she was one, so maybe he had. Before Louise.

"I'll talk to her." Lillian had been meaning to check in with Louise anyway. Louise still hung out and brunched with the other women she had met because they were all dating that guy. She would know some brunch spots for Lillian to add to her lists.

"Good, good. It will be good to see everyone."

Lillian smiled. "It will."

"Also, we should make the soup. So come early," her mom said.

"Okay," Lillian said. She had managed to sneakily document the soup recipe when they made it for Lunar New Year, but she was happy to have another chance.

They said their good byes.

Lillian clicked away from the cactus. Maybe a monstera. Weren't they supposed to relatively easy to care for? She looked around at her messy apartment. It was possible she was not quite ready for plant ownership. Maybe she'd just text her mom that she'd bring dessert.

# Chapter 8

"Xavier! Hey, great minds," Zane said.

"Hey, Zane," Xavier said. The line to pick up pre-ordered food for Thanksgiving was busy this year. They'd asked people to come in designated thirty-minute slots, but they seemed to be running behind or people weren't adhering to their slots, or both. Xavier wasn't in a hurry, they still had an hour before the bar opened, and Bailey was opening today with their newish hire Unika.

"I know you grew up here, is your family getting together tomorrow?" Zane asked.

"My parents don't live here anymore, so we are celebrating separately." Xavier said. "Plus, I'm working both shifts at the bar."

"What are you doing before that?" Zane asked.

Xavier pointed at the line. "Eating all the delicious food."

"Alone?"

Sometimes Xavier wondered if he got a cat, could he then claim he was not eating alone? People made such a big deal about eating alone, but there were things that were really nice about it. All the leftovers were yours. You could eat the food in whatever order you pleased. And no one argued with you about what you watched on TV.

"You should come to my mom's," Zane said, clearly interpreting the silence as a yes. "Louise and my sister and my mom will all be there. The more the merrier and all that."

"That's your family," Xavier shook his head, "you don't need a stranger in there."

"Oh come on, Louise knows you. And if my sister starts trying to tell all my most embarrassing childhood moments to Louise, you can help distract her."

"By asking to hear the embarrassing childhood moments for myself?"

"Okay, seriously, I'm gonna call my mom, but she'll insist."

"Hi, Mom. Yep, I'm in line to pick up the food now. Yes, I made sure to get enough mashed potatoes and extra gravy. Hey, I ran into a friend of mine in line. His family doesn't live here anymore, so he was planning to eat his food all alone."

Xavier shook his head. He noticed Zane didn't mention they had been business partners. He wondered if Zane's mom would be so eager if she knew that part.

"Well, and I know you like to say food tastes better with company. You don't? I could have sworn I heard that from you."

Now Xavier rolled his eyes at Zane. This was very ridiculous.

"I could certainly ask him." Zane looked at Xavier. "My mom wants to know if you would like to join us."

"Sure," Xavier said, because he saw no need to offend Zane's mother who was being very kind. "It's very kind of your mom."

"Okay, Mom, he's very appreciative. Uh, he's right here so, yeah, we will talk about that later. Okay, bye. Yep, two o'clock. I'll tell him."

Xavier had met Zane's Louise before, but not his sister or mom. Zane had mentioned that his mom was not a huge fan of his making a life as a bartender, and kept suggesting he get an office job.

Zane's sister apparently didn't like bars or something. But Xavier could always talk hockey with Louise.

Xavier would have thought after dealing with his parents he'd be better at avoiding awkward invitations. But apparently, he was off his game today. So, he was going to have to make an appearance at this. Maybe he could have Mateo text with an emergency. Though Xavier was just superstitious enough that to think that was asking for trouble. Plus, Zane might want to help. So, fine. He'd dealt with drunken frat boys. He could face one awkward family Thanksgiving dinner with a family that was not his.

"What are you talking about with her later?" Xavier asked.

"Oh, my mom wanted to know if you are single. I'm not sure why. She'll probably forget she asked."

"Okay," Xavier said drawing out the Y. Given Louise and Zane were together, it would seem that Zane's mom wanted to inquire either on behalf of herself or Zane's sister, and Xavier wasn't sure which of those would be more awkward.

# Chapter 9

Lillian carefully balanced the pies as she made her way up her mom's front walk. Her parents had bought this house when downtown Silver Spring had half as many tall buildings as it did now. Even the street they lived on, which growing up had been almost all first and second homeowners, was half turned over, with some of the houses now sporting huge additions taking up half the yard space.

Her parents had done very little to the house while her dad was alive, and her mom hadn't changed much more than the flowers outside. It was a low brick ranch style house. Her mom had turned Lillian's room into an office space. Zane's room still looked like he might be back at any moment.

Lillian rang the doorbell and waited.

"I didn't order any pizzas," her mom said. "Oh, Lillian, why do you have pizza?"

"It's pie, Mom," Lillian said.

"That is a lot of pie. Good thing Zane is bringing a friend," her mom said.

"Louise is more than a friend, Mom," Lillian said maneuvering through the doorway into the house, balancing the boxes. The pumpkin and apple were fine, but the chocolate pecan was wider than the other two for some reason. "Do you want these in the dining room or the kitchen?"

"Kitchen. We'll eat the other food first, then the pie."

Lillian nodded. She put the boxes on the counter and peeked in to make sure each of them still looked okay after that bus ride.

"And I didn't mean the friend Louise. I meant the other one."

"What other one?" Lillian asked.

"Your brother has a friend who is all alone, so he's bringing him to eat here. He wasn't sure if he was single. But you could ask."

"So, Zane is bringing someone and I can ask this person if they are single so that I could what?" Lillian asked. She knew the answer. She just wanted her mom to say it.

"Well, if he's single, you could date him," her mom said. "You should set the table."

Lillian walked over to the silverware drawer. "I should date Zane's friend because why?"

"Because maybe you will like him. Zane likes him."

"Well then Zane can date him." Lillian stating setting the table.

"Zane is already dating someone."

Lillian was half tempted to say, and so what? Because monogamy wasn't the only option, but as much as she wanted to move this discussion in just about any new direction, perhaps discussing non-monogamy was not the move right now.

"So, I have to date this guy, just because Zane is taken? That seems like a weird rule."

"Lillian," her mom said, "you don't have to date anyone. But if you do want to date someone, since I know you had a bad experience before, maybe dating someone Zane already knows would help."

Well, shoot. That was sweet and also, not terrible advice if Lillian was looking for long term right now. She put and arm around her mom's shoulders and squeezed. "Love you, Mom."

"Love you too."

"But you need to lay off my love life."

"Fine, I will say nothing more."

Lillian was quite sure that was a blatant lie. But it was at least likely that her mom would say significantly less things for at least the next hour. Which was something.

"I saw Kermit's mom at the farmer's market on Saturday," Mom said. "She said he's planning on moving back soon."

"Really?" Lillian followed Kermit on social media, but he hadn't been posting a lot lately. Lillian guessed this was why. He'd been having a grand time in Quebec but she wondered if he'd been homesick or something. Lillian still lived in the same town she'd grown up in, but she had gone away to college.

It had been fascinating how many little things you thought were true everywhere, were actually just regional norms. They talked about this a lot in her strategic communications cohort. She, who had never much had strong thoughts about crabs or Old Bay, had begged her parents to send her some Old Bay. She had made popcorn and had teared up a little as she sprinkled it over the popcorn, the smell making her both happy and super homesick all at the same time.

Some of her high school classmates had never come back. Lillian had loved college. She had also been so excited that when it ended, she got to go back home.

They moved back to the kitchen as her mom caught her up on other news. Lillian and her mom started pulling out soup ingredients. Lillian had tried asking her mom what kind of soup it was, but never got a straight answer. This soup had been part of tons of their meals growing up, but then her mom had stopped making it.

Lillian had tried asking her mom for the recipe, but her mom said she had no idea what soup she meant. But for Louise's first Lunar New Year with the family, the soup had been there.

Lillian knew how make this one now, had documented the process enough. She had offered to make it ahead of time, but her mom had hen said if it needed to be made early, she would do it. So now Lillian just came over early and helped her mom make it.

There were root vegetables, squash, ginger, garlic, greens, and miso.

The soup didn't need long to simmer, which was one of the reasons Lillian liked it, in addition is general deliciousness. Zane had once given her a recipe that required like two hours of simmering. She had promptly told him she would just keep raiding his fridge when he made it.

She and her mom finished setting up the table. The table had soup, salad, and wine and water for everyone.

The front door opened and there were voices and sounds as people entered and shed shoes.

Lillian and her mom walked out to the living room. Lillian opened her mouth to tease Zane for just barging in, when the guy next to him turned.

It was Xavier.

Lillian froze and then her heart kicked into gear, pounding hard. She smiled and said, "Hey, I heard you brought another plus one, Zane. Hi, I'm Lillian. Nice to meet you."

Her mouth was ahead of her brain. She hadn't even really formulated the plan to just fake not knowing Xavier, but between Zane's latent patriarchy and her mom's newly discovered matchmaking sensibilities, it did seem the best choice.

Hopefully he would play along.

# Chapter 10

Xavier lived close enough to Zane and Louise that he walked over their place and they all rideshared together with all the food. Zane had said his sister was bringing pie, and his mom would make soup and salad, and they had the food Zane had picked up.

Xavier's parents would both be horrified if he showed up empty handed, so he had brought wine and some chocolate covered macadamia nuts. Growing up his parents had always had a little silver bowl of macadamia nuts out for parties and events. So, while he didn't eat them very often, even though they were much easier to find these days, he kept a stash.

"So," Louise said from her perch in the middle of the backseat, "any questions about the Yang family before we arrive? They only do a few blood rituals. Nothing super weird."

"Louise," Zane said. "She's been binging that new witch academy show and her humor has gotten weird."

"I'm literally right here," Louise said. "Besides, have you ever gone to a strange family's house for Thanksgiving?"

"Well, no, but that doesn't mean we need to joke about blood rituals."

"If it helps," Xavier said, "I thought it was funny."

"See?" Louise said. "Thank you, Xavier. But humor aside, they are nice. And if you wink at me across the table, I'll text you with a fake emergency."

"Can I vote no," Zane asked, "on winking?"

"I thought winking was more subtle than waving, but we can do that if you prefer."

Xavier tried to chuckle quietly. He'd known Zane longer, had worked with him of course, but he found the way Louise was with him fairly hilarious.

"Why would he need a fake emergency?" Zane said.

"Well, hopefully he won't. But sometimes it's easier to have an exit strategy in place."

The driver pulled to a stop.

"Well, we're here," Zane said. "So hopefully we can move on to other subjects."

They thanked the driver and exited the car. Zane handed one of his bags over to Xavier, and got the door open. "We're here!" he called.

They toed their shoes off.

Two figures appeared through the doorway of the cozy living room. The one he assumed was Zane's mom was a short, dark-haired woman in all black clothing. And next to her was Lillian.

She paused looking at him and then smiled and said, " Hey, I heard you brought another plus one, Zane. Hi, I'm Lillian. Nice to meet you."

Um, okay. Xavier nodded and introduced himself, handing Mrs. Yang the wine and macadamia nuts.

"Oh thank you," she said. "Lillian brought very many pies, but these are nice too."

"I'll get this set up," Zane said taking the bags into what Xavier assumed was the kitchen.

"Do you need help?" he asked. He wasn't sure what to do with himself. It had been one thing when he thought he was going to have to make small talk with Zane's mom and sister, over food. Now he was going to have to make small talk with Zane's mom and pretend he had never met Zane's sister. He understood that this was probably just as much of a surprise to Lillian as it was to him, but why not just be like, oh hey, we've met before, small world? Was she embarrassed to have dated or hooked up with him? She was here alone, so assumedly she wasn't married or deeply involved with someone else.

Xavier had been privy to a lot of awkward situations working in a bar, but here wasn't quite sure how to make small talk with someone he was pretending not to have met before. All the things he wanted to say but couldn't crowded up on his tongue. How have you been? Have you wished you had gotten my contact info. Why haven't you been back to Two Bars? Could we at least have sex again one more time? Yeah, that was definitely not appropriate conversation.

Louise and Lillian were talking about - it sounded like yarn - knitting.

"So, Xavier, you grew up here, but your parents are gone?" Mrs. Yang asked.

"Yeah, I grew up in DC, but my parents split up and they each moved away."

"Oh, so they are still alive. Well, that is good," Mrs. Yang said.

"Yeah," Xavier said. He knew Mr. Yang had passed away.

"And you are single?" Mrs. Yang asked.

"Mom!" Lillian said. "I'm sorry," she said to Xavier, "sometimes my mom is a little too nosy."

"How is that nosy?" Mrs. Yang asked. "I'm single, you're single, Louise and Zane are both not single, it's a normal thing to know."

"Hey, Zane," Louise said with her voice raised, "how's that food coming?"

"I think we're ready. Mom, did you put the - oh, there's the ladle. Yep, we're ready."

Mrs. Yang led them into the dining room, and everyone got seated with drinks and soup.

"This soup is really good," Xavier said.

"Lillian helped me make it," Mrs. Yang said. "Both my children enjoy cooking."

"It is really good, Lillian and Mrs. Yang," Louise said.

"I told you you could call me Marian, since you are family now."

Xavier could swear Mrs. Yang glanced over at him as she said that.

"Sorry, Marian."

"No need to be sorry. Xavier, do you like to cook?" Mrs. Yang asked.

"I'm better at eating," Xavier said. "But I tend to work odd hours. So sometimes I have to cook, but I'm more of a functional cook rather than anything particularly interesting."

"Ah, Lillian got more into cooking in the last few years. I think it might have to do with maturity. How old are you?"

"Mom!" Lillian said. "Let's stop quizzing Xavier on his life. How about movies. Has anyone seen a good movie lately?"

"I've been binging 'Academy of Blood' lately," Louise said.

"Yes, she has," Zane said. "So, if anyone has any movie suggestions that do not involve school uniforms and blood rituals, I would love a list."

"Hey," Louise said, "how many times have you watched the fish tank show?"

"No one dies in the fish tank show," Zane said.

"That you know of," Louise said.

"There is a TV show about fish tanks?" Mrs. Yang asked.

"They install fish tanks," Lillian said.

"Okay," Mrs. Yang said. "I still like 'Law and Order'."

"A classic," Xavier said.

Louise made a sound that sounded kind of like "chun chun".

They all looked at her. "Chun chun. Like the sound they make on the show."

When there was silence Xavier tried to help, repeating, "Chun chun."

"Oh, chun chun, yes," Mrs. Yang said. "You are so clever."

Lillian coughed something that sounded suspiciously like "suck up".

A foot knocked into Xavier's under the table and then stayed pressed up against his. He tried to glance underneath, but the table cloth hung long enough to block his view. He was seated next to Mrs. Yang, across from Lillian, and next to Zane. Louise sat diagonal to him and would need very long legs to have reached quite that far. Xavier really hoped that was Lillian. He was hoping somehow they came out of this evening with her interested in seeing him again. In some sort of planned event where they communicated and agreed to be in the same place at the same time.

If it was Zane or Mrs. Yang things got a little more awkward. Zane because Louise didn't strike him as someone into sharing, and Mrs. Yang was a little out of his league.

But because he wasn't sure, he didn't rub his foot back or do anything other than leave it there. As they ate delicious food and talked about TV shows with long runs to binge.

Louse insisted on gathering up plates after they finished food. "Please, I'm the only one who didn't cook anything," she glanced at Xavier, "and doesn't have to work tonight."

"You are working tonight?" Mrs. Yang said.

"Yeah, it's a busy night for bars," Xavier said.

"You work in a bar?"

"Yeah," Xavier said.

"He owns the bar, Mom," Zane said.

"Oh, so you want to check that everyone is working hard," Mrs. Yang said.

That somehow made it sound like he was more of a hands-off owner, like Vance. But maybe now wasn't the time for that discussion.

"I'll be back out with pie in just a moment," Lillian said.

Xavier realized the foot that had been pressed against his was gone, so hopefully that did mean it had been Lillian. Xavier had never quite understood the purpose of footsie. He didn't consider his feet an erogenous zone, so maybe that was why he didn't get excited.

But, if Lillian had been reaching across, or under the table to tell him something, then that meant something. He just wasn't sure what. And it seemed asking in front of her family wasn't a great choice. Somehow, he needed to come away with a way to contact her. He just needed to figure out how to do it, surreptitiously, while sitting at a table full of people.

*\*\**

Lillian had never been filled with so many conflicting emotions. She had once been told to list things, when overwhelmed. Lillian had found that giant lists did not make her feel less overwhelmed. But it was tempting to list things. Nervousness. Horniness. Hunger. For pie. The last was mostly for pie.

"Have you ever been to Xavier's bar?" Louise asked.

Lillian paused grabbing the stack of dessert plates. "Um, no, I haven't." Yeah, that sounded normal and not suspicious. She wanted to bang her head against the cabinet door, but that would also be suspicious.

"It's cool," Louise said. "It's very different vibe from Circle, but I like it. They're open later too, so great for nights when you don't have to get up early the next day."

Or for people who worked in the food industry and didn't start until later for the most part. Or shift workers of all kinds. Even the execs at Lillian's company sometimes wanted to know where they could take people who were arriving on a late flight, or after they'd gotten out of long day of meetings.

It was a smart business choice. Lillian wasn't surprised. His observations about Two Bars had been on point. She wondered if he had been back. If he had looked for her. If he had been happy to see her today. Of course, her pretending she had never met him was why she didn't now know the answer to this. Really annoying, the consequences of her own actions doing her in like that. Rude, even.

"But they don't do cocktails," Louise said. "Or nothing with like more than two ingredients. So mostly beer, wine, and shots. Schism," Louise lowered her voice, "did more. It's a shame that didn't work out."

"Xavier was part of Schism?" Lillian asked also keeping her voice low.

"Yep, it was his idea. He asked Zane to be his partner."

Lillian had been to Schism, but she didn't remember meeting Xavier. And she would not have forgotten him. She shut the dishwasher carefully.

"Do you need help with the plates?" Louise asked.

Right, plates. "No, I think I can handle five plates. But thanks."

"You're welcome."

Louise gave her a searching look, and Lillian smiled and walked back into the dining room, walking around and placing plates in front of everyone. She accidentally inhaled leaning over Xavier and the hit of whatever scent he wore made her a little warm inside.

"What kind of pie did you bring?" her mom asked.

Lillian talked through the pies and they each grabbed some.

Lillian sat back down at her seat and her plate made a small odd sound. She lifted the plate back up, and spotted a small piece of paper.

"Something wrong?" Mom asked.

"Nope," Lillian said. "Just forgot to move my napkin." Her napkin was already in her lap, but hopefully her mom wouldn't notice that. Lillian snagged the paper with the hand not nearest her mom, and tucked it into her jeans. If it was stray receipt that had fallen out of the pie box, she was going to be disappointed.

Disappointed that she had wasted all that subterfuge of course. She still didn't date bartenders. Or people her mom tried to set her up with. Or folks who had worked with her brother, which was the entire reason for the bartender rule in the first place.

"Well, I hate to eat and run, but I gotta get going," Xavier said. "Thanks to all of you for letting me crash your holiday dinner."

"Thanks to you," Louise said, "for letting Zane, uh, invite you."

"It was very nice to have you join us," Mom said.

"Yeah," Lillian smiled and nodded.

"You should take home some pie. Lillian brought too much," Mom said.

"I brought the right amount," Lillian muttered.

Her mom came back from the kitchen with plastic ware, and made Xavier take some soup and some pie with him. They waved him off and then came back to survey the dining room.

"I can clear up this round of dishes," Zane said.

"We need to put some of this away," Mom said. "Most of it."

They got everything cleared and stowed in the fridge. The pies they left out.

They moved into the living room where Zane found the hockey game on TV.

"They play hockey on holidays?" Mom asked.

"Oh yeah," Louise said. "They usually take a small break around Christmas, but there's games for Canadian Thanksgiving, American Thanksgiving, and of course New Year's."

"So, Louise," Mom said. "Maybe you know someone for Lillian to date."

"Mom!" Lillian said. "Please stop."

"I was just asking. You will decide whatever choice makes the most sense for you."

It was a holiday, so Lillian, in the interest of family harmony, did not mention this was at least the third time she had asked her mom to stop, so clearly it was not entirely up to Lillian.

"I did not have a lot of success finding people to date," Louise said. "Zane was kind of an accident."

"Um, hello?" Zane said.

"Oh, you know what I mean. I had a whole plan, and you were not it. Obviously, the plan was flawed."

"Or," Zane nudged her with his elbow, "the plan was perfect because it led you to me."

Lillian made a gagging noise.

When they all stared at her, she said, "Sorry, hairball. You know I love you, Louise."

"What about me?" Zane said.

"You make great soup. I love that about you," Lillian said.

"You made great soup today, Lillian," her mom said.

"Thanks, Mom. You too," Lillian said.

"Do you think Xavier got enough to eat? It sounds like he works very hard."

"I think he'll be okay, Mom," Zane said.

"Oh no!" Louise said. "Sorry, hockey oh no."

Later, when they packed up to go, Lillian hugged her mom. "Bye, mom. You sure you don't want any of the pie?"

"No, I ate plenty. I'm fine. You can always go share some with Xavier, if you want."

"Bye, Mom," Lillian said.

Louise and Zane walked out the door with her. "We can get the rideshare to drop you home, if you want," Louise said.

"No, I'm fine. I'm gonna walk. Then I'll be ready for more pie later."

"Well, text us when you get home," Louise said.

They all hugged as the rideshare car pulled up. Lillian waved to them, and then started walking home. The pie remainders fit nicely into a bag that was much more maneuverable than it had been on her way up.

Lillian got home and texted Louise and Zane. And then after she pulled out the piece of paper, she grabbed herself a piece of pie and then added the phone number to her phone. Should she text him now, or wait until tomorrow. Probably tomorrow. He'd be slammed tonight anyway. She should have asked what bar he worked at. Now it would be weird if she asked Louise or Zane.

Louise wouldn't think anything of it. But she would tell Zane. And then Zane would want it to be a group outing. And no one wanted their sibling along while they were trying to hookup. She quickly googled. And got back Bottom's Up, which, she checked the address, was really close to Two Bars.

Excellent. She could stop in tonight and see if anything happened. If it did, it would still be just a hookup. She still didn't want a relationship. And she still didn't date bartenders. But maybe hookups weren't dating. She wasn't breaking the rule. Just refining it a little.

# Chapter 11

Xavier stopped in at Two Bars. He had been at Bottom's Up last night well after close, because a number of glasses had broken. He had needed to rearrange his office to access the case of replacement glasses. He needed a better system in there.

But seeing Lillian had reminded him of Della.

"Hey, there," Della said. "Still haven't seen her."

"I actually saw her yesterday," Xavier said. "I wanted to ask you a question. A professional one."

"Oooh, okay. Let me seat you at the business end of the bar here, and get these folks all topped up."

Xavier settled in, and thanked Della for both the water and the beer she brought him before she made her way down the line. The bar wasn't crowded yet. Xavier was willing to bet at least one of the couples was staying in a short-term rental nearby and had just googled bars nearby to end up here. They had a certain we came all this way to see our family and now we need some alcohol kind of shell-shocked look.

Family holidays in the DC area were an interesting mix. Since a portion of the city were transplants from elsewhere, a number of people went somewhere else for the holidays. But a large number of people also either came back here for the holidays, or convinced their family to come check out the city for the holiday. November wasn't normally considered a big tourism month, there were often a lot of newbies to the city.

Della came back down to his end of the bar.

"So, what have you got?"

"Well, I know you're here, and I don't want to mess with that. But I do have a staff member who is going to be reducing her hours. So, if you wanted to pick up extra shifts or something, I'd be happy to add you to our schedule. The commute would be about the same."

"You guys open later and close later?"

"We do," Xavier said. "You could certainly stop by tonight, or some other night if you wanted to get a sense for things. We're closed Monday and Tuesday, but other than that."

"I will definitely think about that. You just have the one place?" Della asked.

"Yeah, just one," Xavier said. He and Zane had done their best to find all the employees of Schism a job, had given everybody references. Schism had been more restaurant, more family oriented, and so not all of the old employees wanted to work in a bar with late hours, or were even trained for bartending. Bottom's Up didn't do fancy cocktails or anything like that, but there was still a different rhythm to bar service. Not everybody liked it. And the hours of course, meant staff had to either be willing to bus or rideshare home, since they were open past metro's last trains.

"Alright, do you need another drink?" Della asked.

"No, I'm all set. Thank you for hearing me out, Della."

"Of course. And you have a good shift tonight. I may stop by."

Xavier smiled and put some cash on the bar, tucking it under the glass.

Bailey was already at Bottom's Up when he arrived. They went through the bar, getting things open. Mateo and Dan were both scheduled to show up later, along with Zane having said to call if thing got crowded and they needed him earlier.

They opened up and customers began trickling in. The dishwasher hose kept sticking, and he had run back to make sure he could get it going. It finally started. When he came back to the bar, Lillian was seated there.

He had no idea when she had arrived, or how she had managed to score a seat, but this was great.

"You got my number, right?" he asked.

"Hello to you too," Lillian said. "And yeah, I did. But Louise told me such wonderful things about this place, I figured I would check it out."

"Glad to have you. And hello. Do you need a drink?"

"I got wine for her," Bailey said, sliding it down.

"Oh good," Xavier said. One of the customers waved for a refill. "Okay, I'll be back."

"I'll be here," Lillian said.

He went and helped the waving customer. There was a period of nonstop orders where he and Bailey were just stacking them up. Other than the stools right up against the bar, much of the customer area in Bottom's Up was standing room. It meant they could pack in a big crowd, though things were not so big right now that they had to worry about capacity.

He looked over at Lillian a few times while pouring drinks, and she smiled back each time. He brought her another wine when he noticed hers was low.

"Oh thank you," she said. "So, is it always this busy?"

"This is the holiday crowd, so this is extra busy."

"Wow," Lillian said.

Her phone on the bar flashed.

"Gotta watch that," he said. "Phone in the splash zone."

"Oh, I'm sure it's...okay, Louise and Zane are headed here, so that is my cue to go. Can I close out my tab?"

"Sure," Xavier said. He brought her the receipt and kept all the questions about why Louise and Zane being here meant she had to leave inside. It wasn't likely to slow down much tonight, so it wasn't like they were going to have time to really chat. "Well, you can come back some other night. Or of course you have my number."

"Yep, I do," Lillian said. She grabbed her stuff and walked off. Someone immediately slid into her stool and ordered a drink so he didn't even get to finish watching her walk away from him. Again.

# Chapter 12

Lillian probably owed Xavier an explanation. And any minute now, her master strategic communications skills were going to kick in and she would figure out what that was. Like I don't date bartenders but I wanted to see you? I don't date bartenders, but maybe you are planning to quit and also never talk to my brother again? I don't date bartenders, but maybe we could just have repeated one-night stands?

She shouldn't go see him again until she had figured out what she wanted. Annoying.

Louise: Up for girl brunch?

Lillian: Sure! When are you thinking?

She sincerely hoped Louise did not mean now since Lillian was currently still lying in bed, probably still smelling like the bar.

They settled on an hour at a place that located between them, and had open reservations.

Lillian arrived with wet hair piled up in a bun, and just a few minutes late. So like basically on time. Lillian liked to consider being a tiny bit late, her own personal pushback against the model minority stereotype.

"So, you didn't want to check out Xavier's place?" Louise said after they had put in their orders.

"Oh, no, I just, well, there were things," Lillian said. She should have prepared a better explanation. "Besides, Zane gets a little weird when I befriend his bartender friends." Okay technically that had only happened once. Well, twice. And a third time that Zane didn't know about.

"Does he? Fascinating. Wait, do you mean, befriend, or like befriend," Louise asked.

Lillian shrugged.

"And are you going to befriend Xavier?" Louise asked. "Because, Xavier does not tell me much about himself, but I've never known him to date like anyone. I could ask the other folks at Bottom's Up, but I kinda think they'd say the same. Cady might know. Cady knows very many things."

Lillian laughed. Cady managed Circle, and Cady did seem to know very many things. Lillian was very careful about what she said around Cady.

"Yes, well, my mother decided I should date someone Zane knows. And Zane historically has not been a fan of that, so it does make achieving family harmony a bit of a puzzle."

"I noticed your mom quizzing him. So that's new for her, for you?"

"Brand new. I'm sorry to say I think it's all your fault, you've made Zane happy so therefore, I can only be happy if I couple up."

"Sorry, not sorry though." Louise said. "But to be clear, if you want to befriend, date, couple up, or not couple up, that's obviously for you to decide. Not your mom and not Zane."

"I know." And Lillian did know. But she appreciated Louise saying it.

"I know you know, but I also know family pressure can be a lot to overcome. And Zane can get right over himself if he has a problem dating someone he liked enough to partner up with for business."

"How long have they known each other?" Lillian asked.

"Oh, a while. And then Xavier asked Zane to be his partner for Schism. It was such a great idea to. The pandemic just came at the wrong time. I mean, there's not really a great time for a pandemic. But I think if they had been open a little longer, they'd have been able to weather it. Maybe not, the landlord was kind of a jerk about it. Like I guess landlords need to be paid too, but he was unwilling to work with them, and actually threatened to sue them."

"I hadn't realized it was that dire," Lillian said. Zane had sort of downplayed things.

"Eh, the landlord was mostly hot air. And fortunately, they got a loan big enough to cover the rental payments and the staff payouts. But like the landlord didn't know that. And it wasn't like they were trying to skip payments. They were just feeling out if the landlord was willing to engage in a profit-sharing model. Obviously, the answer was no."

This helped explain why Xavier was so knowledgeable about the scene. Running one bar would do it. But having experience running and closing a restaurant helped.

"Well, anyway," Lillian said, because she was going to spend more time thinking about Xavier, at home, away from supportive people who were likely to tell her brother things, "what's your book club reading this month?"

"Oh, it's a cute witchy story, small town, Jersey Shore witches."

"Oh fun. I'll need the title of course. I'm going to put in an order with the bookstore soon."

"Nice."

"I know. It's very silly, but when I pre-order and they package it all up for me, it feels like I'm getting a present. Even though I know what's inside."

"No, but that makes sense. Picking up packages is fun. Plus, then you don't get distracted by all the other things."

"Oh no, I almost always buy other things when I go in. But at least I know I got the books I meant to get, and didn't forget them and only bring home cards, a coloring book, and some cute socks."

Louise laughed. "Are you coloring now too?"

"I am not. Though I do have a full set of pencils," Lillian said. "Pretty much sticking to knitting these days."

"Oh, how are your knitting ladies?"

Lillian decided not to mention they were also Team Couple Lillian Up, lest Louise rescind her your choice stance. "They are doing well. Well, mostly. Torrey's got some stuff going on with her partner. I should check, they were going to try some suggestions I put together for them for date nights."

"Wait, are you like a date night concierge now? Because Zane and I mostly hang at Circle, and Bottom's Up. Oh, and the soup place. We could definitely use some suggestions. Well, probably date day suggestions, since he works most nights except Monday, and I am never up for date night on Monday, sadly."

"Not officially no. But some of the execs like to ask me for restaurant and other suggestions. And so, I keep track of a lot of that stuff, and it means I can come up with suggestions pretty easily. I could come up with some stuff for you guys. You could always pick a museum with a good restaurant in it. Get a little culture, eat some food."

"I always forget about all the museums. That's a great idea."

Lillian might put together a few more suggestions for them and send them later. She'd text Torrey too. And Xavier. As soon as she figured out what to say to him.

# Chapter 13

"Happy Hawaiian Independence Day!" Xavier's mom said.

"Happy Hawaiian Independence Day to you too," Xavier said. He was a little confused. Because for one, Hawai'i was not, what you call independent these days. His mom had grown up in Hawai'i but had gone to college in DC, and stayed. Well, until she left for New York.

They had gone to visit relatives in Hawai'i when he was a kid, but only every few years. They had read Hawaiian stories, and of course watched movies about Hawai'i. His mom had demanded to see his history book in high school to make sure the overthrow of the Hawaiian monarchy and subsequent annexation was covered correctly. She had decided it was not, and so had made him talk to his grandmother about it. And every once in a while, his mom would call with a new thing they were supposed to do or acknowledge as Hawaiian people.

Xavier always appreciated learning about new traditions or events. But it was always a little odd when his mom sprung a new one on him,

"Remind me, how does one celebrate the independence of a formerly independent nation?" he asked keeping his tone as neutral as possible.

"Oh, who knows, probably by drinking, and tossing a lei into a bonfire."

"Ah," Xavier said. "I will look into getting a lei tomorrow." Xavier winced a little. It was clear what he meant, but that was a weird phrase to say to one's mother.

"There's actually a lei maker in DC. I saw segment about her on the news. Support small businesses!"

Xavier resisted reminding his mother that he was himself running a small business. People usually did not think of bars as being small business but they were. Well, some of them were. Some of them were own by huge conglomerates, or, Vance. "I know her," Xavier said.

Adriana the lei maker was dating Zane's friend Seth. They tended to hang at Circle rather than Bottom's Up, but he and Adriana had gone to the Kamehameha ceremony at the Capitol along with her friend Kai.

"So, no fireworks, maybe alcohol, but buy a lei and support small businesses," he said.

"I'm sure there's alcohol involved."

"Makes sense," Xavier said smiling. Most independence type days seemed to be celebrated with alcohol. Since alcohol was Xavier's business, he could hardly object. He was not going to do Hawaiian specials at the bar however. He didn't hide being Hawaiian, but it was the kind of thing people got weird about. Especially when they'd been drinking. Everything from talking about their luxury vacations, to being surprised that the palace was an actual palace and not a hut, to insisting that putting pineapple or an umbrella on a drink made it tropical.

Xavier had a love/hate relationship with the idea that every few years, some white dude who had a mind-blowing beach vacation would open some sort of tiki bar. It tended to involve torches, lots of rum drinks, and oddly appropriative decor. The bar staff would wear floral shirts that they insisted on calling Hawaiian shirts, though it took more than florals to make something Hawaiian.

It would usually be the hot new thing for about six weeks, and then a year later they would rebrand as something else.

DC used to have a really good Hawaiian restaurant, but it had closed the prior summer.

"So, what else have you been up to?" his mother asked.

"Working for the most part," he said. He was pretty sure mentioning he went to Zane and Lillian's mom house would lead to a lecture on spending family holidays with your real family.

"So much work. You should get a lei tomorrow. It will give you an excuse to go somewhere that is not work."

"I will do that," Xavier said, meaning he would order one, since he suspected getting lei involved lead time. "Have you been up to anything interesting lately?"

"Oh you know, this and that. We're in the middle of a big merger at work. Lots of meetings and policy discussions."

"Have you been somewhere that is not work lately?" Xavier asked.

"Oh, you're so sweet to worry about me. I have. I have. But also, I have a social circle and neighbors I talk to."

Xavier had a social circle. Yes, many of them he had met through work, and okay, some of them worked for him right now. He also talked to his neighbor, Ms. Francie. He waved at his other neighbor. And okay, maybe he needed a hobby or something, but his mother's hobby was going to city council meetings which sounded a lot like work you just didn't get paid for. Xavier dealt with the city all the time, between neighborhood commissions, and alcohol boards, and fire inspections. He felt very connected to the city government and was not interested in dedicating more time to it.

After he and his mother hung up, he googled Hawaiian Independence Day. He was pretty sure his mother was not super pro-sovereignty land back, which seemed to be the primary reason folks were trying to bring the holiday back. His mom was very proud of her Hawaiian roots, but tended to be in favor of the more center, let's work with the structure we have now, kind of person.

But while he was aware his Hawaiian-ness was not a video game with energy that dropped and needed to be topped up, it always felt good to connect with a piece of it. This time of year was so busy, that sometimes just pondering something else was a little refreshing. He could do a toast tonight after close. But there would definitely not be an umbrella in the drink.

# Chapter 14

Lillian was having trouble figuring out what to eat for dinner, which was throwing off her whole plan for the evening. She should have ordered something like forty minutes ago, but now everything was saying it would take an hour to arrive, and she was ready to gnaw her arm off now. She could of course, go grab something somewhere. But she was still in a bra and because she tended to be a messy eater and didn't want to put her shirt on before she ate. It was easier clean herself rather than her get lucky top.

But fine. She threw the get lucky top on. It was black, and had a square neck, and a shelf bra. The shelf bra, actual bra combo made her boobs look fantastic, and paired with her favorite slim cut jeans she had never not scored on a night she was in the mood to score. And tonight she had decided, she and Xavier didn't really need words, they were better without words. Words were just the tools to get them back where they were best.

She managed, with the help of like seven napkins, not to spill any pizza on herself. She checked herself in the phone camera. Yep, looked great. She was ready to get to Bottom's Up and enact Operation Hookup. The name lacked imagination, but it was clear and to the point. She had condoms in her purse, a metro card, a phone, and lipstick, and a face mask. She was ready to go.

The bus however was not. Well, in fairness to the bus and the driver, it was the four emergency vehicles blocking the roadway that were keeping the bus from going. The driver exited the bus, to try and find out what was going on. He came back and said, "Yeah folks, there's an accident and they don't know when it's going to clear."

Lillian looked, traffic was stacked behind them, and the bus was stopped in the middle of the block, just behind all the emergency vehicles, so there was no easy way for the bus to detour. Several people got up and started filing off the bus. Lillian checked the time. Bottom's

Up didn't close for another two hours. So, she still had time. But also, she could walk to the bar in far less than two hours. The weather was chilly tonight, but she had worn her puffer coat, the better to unzip and reveal the get lucky shirt. She'd be okay. She got up and wished the bus driver luck.

Six blocks later, it became clear the part of her plan she hadn't thought about was the shoes. She was wearing ballet flats, and she didn't usually do a whole lot of walking in these. She had walked enough that her feet had started sweating. And now she had a blister. The bar was only about three blocks more, so she'd make it. But hobbling was not quite the look she had been going for.

Lillian paused once she made it to the block Bottom's Up sat on. As she waited for the light to cross, she took a deep breath and reminded herself that she, was cute, she was sexy, and the lucky shirt had never failed.

She walked into the bar and saw Mateo and Bailey. The bar had a number of people gathered, but wasn't packed like it had been last time.

Lillian ordered a wine and sat down. Xavier had said he was a workaholic. She supposed he could have already worked and gone home. He lived near enough that they could always call him if something happened.

Lillian waited until her second glass of wine to ask Mateo. "So, is Xavier around tonight?"

"We bullied him into taking a night off. But he'll probably accidentally wander by, because he won't be able to help himself."

"He better not," Bailey said. "Wait, what was your name again?" Bailey gave her a piercing stare that had Lillian sitting up a little straighter in response.

"Lillian," she said with a friendly smile.

"Oh, hey, Lillian."

Lillian turned and saw Della behind her. "Hey, Della! It's great to see you...well, when you aren't working, I guess."

"It's nice to be not working, though it was slow tonight. Guess you decided to bug Xavier at work." Della pulled up next to Lillian and gave Bailey her order.

"Xavier's not here at the moment," Lillian said.

"Ah, well, that's not surprising he is the boss and all," Della said.

It wasn't any of Lillian's business, but also, she felt a tad defensive on behalf of the absent Xavier. "I think they made him take a night off," Lillian said.

"Who - Xavier?" Mateo said, sliding Della's drink to her. "Yeah, we bullied him. He worked like every shift last week."

"So, he's kind of a micromanager then?" Della asked with a studied casualness.

"No," Bailey said. "But he always wants us to have work life balance. So when we have a week where everything's packed, and we need more help, he's usually the one who picks up a lot of the slack. Then we have to remind him all the stuff he tells us about having a life outside of the bar so he will go home. Or not here. Are you the bartender at Two Bars?"

"I am," Della said.

"She's great," Lillian said.

Della smiled. "I heard you all might need some additional staff."

"We do," Bailey said. "I'm pregnant, so I'm cutting my hours. Not because anyone's making me, but because between the doctor's appointments and the swollen feet I just can't - well, I could, I don't want to work a full schedule here. Plus, I'm going to take time off once the baby's born. My sweetie works in the restaurant industry too, and there aren't exactly a lot of day cares that are set up for restaurant hours. So, we're going to have to figure out a plan for that too."

"Congrats on the pregnancy," Lillian said. "Congrats seems like such a weird thing to say, but like yay."

Bailey smiled. "Yeah, congrats somehow makes it feel like I leveled up or something. But it is something people say, so we'll go with it."

"I work in communications," Lillain said, "so sometimes my brain overanalyzes all the words. Carry on with your job interview."

"Yeah, Bailey," Xavier said, "carry on with the job interview."

"Hi, Boss," Mateo said with a suck up smile.

Lillian couldn't help giggling a little at him.

"Well, Xavier," Bailey said, "we covered why there was an opening in our staff. We were getting to the why are you seeking new or additional employment part, but she works at Two Bars, so that question was kind of a formality." She looked back at Della. "One thing you should know, part of the reason Xavier is often here, is because he doesn't believe in staffing anyone alone for a shift. Not even when we first open on Wednesday or Sunday when it's usually slow. So, if someone calls out, he shows up to cover until we get someone else. It makes peeing during your shift much easier."

Della nodded.

"And by the way, I need a bio break. But you two can handle things for two minutes, right?"

Mateo nodded. He waited until Bailey disappeared in back before stage whispering, "She's bossy but mostly harmless."

"I don't mind bossy when people know what they are bossing about," Della said. "I can be a bit bossy myself, which is why I didn't mind the idea of working alone."

"Yeah, I can see that," Mateo said. "Sounds cool until you have to pee or replace the keg when you have a customer who you just know is gonna try something the minute you're out of their sight. Like that guy, was it last week, or the week before, who had read the article about tipping the kegs to get the ideal ratio of air in there. And so, he wanted to hop behind the bar to show us."

"I think he was like three weeks ago. I haven't seen him back," Xavier said. "Though it was probably too packed last week for him to try climbing over the bar."

Xavier glanced over and paused. "Lillian, hi."

"Hi," she said smiling. She had sort of assumed that while he'd been hovering behind them, he had spotted her. But apparently, she was a surprise. A good one she assumed.

"Hey, Boss, I had a genius idea," Mateo said.

Bailey snorted.

"What if Della shadows us tonight, through closing. And then you could go back home and maybe also make sure Lillian gets safely, uh, home."

"Okay," Bailey said. "I take it back, that is a great idea. If you were planning to stick through closing, Della."

"Okay, but if she's working -" Xavier said.

"I'm up for it," Della said.

"And I will get her to fill out all the stuff, so you can add her to the payroll," Bailey said.

"Oh, well, I still haven't-" Della said.

"You can still say no, Della," Xavier said. "Even if you help them close tonight. But if you work, we're gonna pay you."

"Okay, then sure, I'm up for it," Della said.

Lillian handed Mateo cash. And stood up, grabbing her coat from the stool.

"I guess you're being kicked out of the bar," Xavier said on the sidewalk, as if he had finally figured out what had happened. "I'm not sure that's great customer service on our part."

"I'm not offended," Lillian said. "I had maybe not very subtly asked if you were going to be there."

"Well, normally I would have been. But I let my staff send me home."

"And then you came back. You really are a workaholic," Lillian said.

"Yeah, well, truth in advertising, I guess. So you were looking for me. Does this mean we should take my staff's advice and go back to my place."

"That sounds like a great idea," Lillian smiled. The get lucky shirt scores again.

# Chapter 15

Owning a bar meant things changed quickly. You could turn around to find people about to throw a punch, about to have sex, and all sort of things in between. Lillian showing up tonight was somehow more unexpected than finding Della there being de facto job interviewed by Bailey. He basically expected Bailey to interview people. And if Della hadn't met Bailey's standards she'd probably have been gone before Xavier showed up.

It's possible the Della interview had distracted Bailey long enough that she hadn't gotten around to interviewing Lillian. He knew it all came from a place of love. Much of his staff had worked there for years, they were protective of the space, and protective of each other. Even the ones who had gone onto other things like Tomas and Emilia.

But all the staffing problems were for another day. Well, tomorrow at least. Since Lillian was here now. And not planning to disappear tonight.

He opened the door to his place and gestured for her to go inside. She toed off her shoes and shook out one foot.

"Are you okay?" he asked.

"Just a blister. No biggie," she said.

"Okay. Do you need water or something else to drink. I definitely have water and coffee. Not sure what else I have."

"I'm good," Lillian said. "I was going to text you to explain but, I decided," she stepped closer to him, "that it was easier to explain in person."

"Uh-huh," Xavier said. "Can I kiss you?"

Lillian pressed forward and their lips met, and all of Xavier's thoughts became focused on puller her closer, tighter. Their bodies pressed together, and his tongue met hers as he moved one hand to the hem of her shirt, pulling, tugging until he got to skin. He felt her hands tugging on his t-shirt and he pulled back so she could pull it off. And he grabbed hers. "May I?"

"Please," she said.

He tugged off her shirt, and then started moving back towards his bedroom, shucking jeans, and boxers, and grabbing the box of condoms still sitting on the dresser.

Xavier wanted to go both slow and fast. He wanted all the things, and he wanted this moment to last forever.

"Were you thinking fast this first time or slow?"

Xavier wanted to go both slow and fast. He wanted all the things, and he wanted this moment to last forever.

"Were you thinking fast this first time or slow?"

"Fast. Please," Lillian said.

He slid the condom on, then climbed onto the bed. And Lillian followed and he helped her straddle him, slid down on him, and stroked her ass as she started moving over and on him. He watched her face as she picked up speed, watching her shift, and moan as she changed the angle. He reached between them, stroking her clit. She braced her hands on his shoulders, and moved faster. He felt the orgasm building and squeezed her hip, urging her on.

She exploded above him, and he followed not long after. She relaxed her arms, laying against him.

A few moments, or many, he had kind of lost all track of time, she shifted. "Let me let you up," she said.

He grabbed the base of the condom and she slid off. He sat up and paused, "You can stay. Please stay."

"Okay," she said.

He nodded and walked into the bathroom to toss the condom in the trash. He wanted to cuddle her, he wanted to watch her come again and again, and he wanted them to talk about how they could date or something that wasn't her showing up and then disappearing again. He wanted.

He walked back into the bedroom and she was curled up facing the door, fast asleep. He carefully tugged the duvet from underneath her, and then climbed onto the bed and pulled it over both of them. He pulled her close and she seemed to sigh, though that might have been wishful thinking on his part. Tomorrow. They could talk tomorrow.

# Chapter 16

Lillian reached out to slap her alarm and got a handful of shoulder. Right. Xavier.

"Your phone, I'm guessing?" he said.

"Yeah, sorry." Her alarm was set to get louder by increments. It kind of sounded like they were very close to it switching from the pretty music to the klaxon. She needed to get up and get it, but she was naked and she could tell it was cold. It was much more fun to press her naked self against Xavier's naked self.

The alarm switched to klaxon and she reluctantly slid out and skipped out into the living area to grab her phone and make it snooze. She checked her work calendar. Her first meeting wasn't until ten, and it was now, eight, so she just needed to get home, and get a new shirt on, and she'd be good. She yawned. She really wanted more sleep.

Well, she thought as she watched Xavier wander in still naked, more him wouldn't be half bad either.

"Coffee?" Xavier asked. "Do you need to go? I maybe have cereal."

"I could probably take coffee like to go. Oh gosh, that sounds so entitled, like please make mine to go. So basically, yes, I need to go, but this was great. And thanks for letting me stay." Lillian wasn't sure why she sounded like a comment card all of a sudden. A generic Airbnb review. We had a great time! 5 stars.

"I know you have work, but we should chat about things at some point. I am on shift at the bar tonight, but you could always come over - either to the bar, or to here if you wanted."

Lillian started putting on her clothes. "So let me check with you once I see how the workday goes."

"You've got my number?" he asked.

"Oh, yes." She grabbed her phone and pulled up the contact of his. It was tempting to snap a picture of him naked to put in her contacts. Okay actually, she wasn't really going to save it as her contact photo for him, but she snapped a quick picture. And then she opened his contact and texted him.

Lillian: It's me, Lillian.

She realized if he was naked, his phone was, she looked around the room, probably in his pants over there. "I texted you, so you have my info too. But if not tonight, I have knit night tomorrow, but like are you working at the bar Friday and Saturday too?"

"Yep," he said. "Oh, I do have cereal." He pulled a box out of a kitchen cabinet. He frowned at it.

From where Lillian was sitting it looked like Halloween themed cereal which was hilarious and something she would ponder later. Lillian scanned the room, making sure she had everything but her shoes which were by the door. The rest of the clothes scattered across the floor looked to be his. She grabbed her purse and slid on her coat. She wanted to kiss him again but was afraid she wouldn't be able to just kiss him, so she zipped up her coat and said, "Okay, I'll text you". And slid on her shoes and slipped out the door.

Morning after walks were so much easier with a coat. Plus, Lillian was pretty sure her makeup was all gone now. She pulled out her phone and checked the selfie cam. She had seen enough weird things on metro, that even if her makeup had been smeared across her face, she was pretty sure she'd barely be a blip on most people's radar. But no, there were still faint lipstick remnants on her lips, but otherwise she looked fine. she clicked the icon to go into her gallery and started to click on the picture of Xavier before realizing she was on the metro and people could see her screen.

She could look at it later. After she showered and changed and put in a day of work. And figured out what to text Xavier, and what she should tell him about how they should definitely sleep together and also definitely not tell Zane or Louise, or like anyone who knew them. Well, Mateo and Bailey already knew, or suspected. Had she already blown the secrecy?

Would it be weird for Xavier to tell his employees not to tell anyone he was dating. Or that he was dating her? That was probably too weird. She just - it wasn't worth seeing if Zane had learned and grown. It was easier to not tell him. Then he didn't have to stretch himself, and she didn't have to be annoyed with him, or have Louise get annoyed with him. If he was a jerk, he would deserve people being annoyed, but also, they could skip it all.

Plus, with her mom on the couple everyone up kick, she needed no one, not even the knitting folks to know what was going on. The cone of silence already had people in it.

And okay, if Lillian found this secret relationship thing a little fun, like playing footsie under the table at dinner fun, well, why shouldn't she get to indulge that. Secrets were fun. More people should try keeping secrets instead of spilling them.

# Chapter 17

Lillian: Hey, super busy day. And I need to catch up on sleep. But can I call you before you head to work?

Xavier's stomach dropped.

Xavier: Sure.

The call came through a hot second later.

"Hey," Lillian said.

"Hey," he said. She had only said one word, but the sound of her voice had his shoulders relaxing even as other parts started paying extra attention.

"So, I was thinking," Lillian said. "If it's okay with you, I would rather keep things between us. Zane is sometimes a little annoying about who I, uh, date, so if it's not weird, I would rather not tell him. Or Louise. Louise wouldn't care, but she would want to tell Zane."

Xavier rubbed a spot on the kitchen counter. "I don't want to lie to Zane." One things Xavier had learned from all the stuff with his parents, was that lies just beget more lies. It was easier to tell the truth.

"Do you have to lie, or could you just not mention me by name, maybe," Lillian said. "Like I don't want you to do anything you're uncomfortable with, but I like to keep my family separate from everything else. It's just easier. For everyone."

Xavier wasn't sure why this rubbed him the wrong way. Lillian was right that he did not normally share anything about his dating status or lack thereof with Zane. He could continue to talk with Zane about other stuff and not mention Lillian. And he certainly wasn't planning to tell either of his parents about Lillian right now. And he had met Lillian's family and had no current plans to reciprocate by introducing her to any of his family. So, it was like she said, less of a secret, more of a perfectly normal separation of work and family. He was friendly with Zane sure, but technically they were colleagues. Zane was part of his work life. So not telling Zane about his not work life, was less hiding, more keeping things professional.

"Um, okay," he said. "Though I can't speak for Mateo and Bailey."

"Yeah, and like to be clear, it's not that I think us, um, dating is like a bad thing. Well, dating isn't really the right word, but the point is, I'm not like ashamed of anything. I just - Zane sometimes thinks he's helping me, and in fact he is not helping. Keeping him out of range is best all around. If that makes sense."

Xavier hadn't even thought she might be ashamed, but now he wondered. He knew Zane's parents hadn't initially loved the idea of him working as a bartender. They'd wanted him to stick to more of an office job.

But Mrs. Yang hadn't seemed bothered by him being a bar owner. But of course, she hadn't known he was going to date Lillian. And he still wasn't sure if they realized he was the one who had partnered with Zane. If they blamed him for that. So yeah, maybe keeping the Lillian parts of his life distinct from the Zane parts of his life was good planning.

"Well, I'm sure you need to get ready for work, so I'll let you go. But I'll stop by Friday or Saturday."

"I work closing both of those nights."

"I'll drink coffee beforehand," Lillian said.

Xavier smiled. See, everything was going to be fine.

# Chapter 18

"Ugh, I forgot we have the hospital tour tomorrow," Bailey said sitting on the stool next to Lillian. It was early Wednesday evening, so things were pretty slow. Just Lillian and a few other patrons so far. All regulars.

"What is a hospital tour?" Lillian asked. "Like I can imagine, but why do you need to tour the hospital? Do you get to be like no, actually, we're going to book a different one with a better caterer?"

Bailey chuckled. "Wouldn't that be nice. My ob/gyn has privileges in two hospitals, and Tomas wants to look at both of them before we officially decide. The one tomorrow is in DC, but it's upper northwest so it's like a pain in the ass to get there on public transit. Sorry, Mr. Watkins, pain in the butt."

Mr. Watkins turned on his stool, giving up any pretense that he wasn't listening. "You can swear. I tend not to, but that's a choice for me, not for you. Is this hospital well rated for pregnant people? I know you all like your ratings."

Bailey smiled. "It is well rated. My doctor's also got privileges in Takoma, but it's farther from transit. Once I'm in labor, we'll rideshare, but Tomas will likely have to go back and forth a few times, so transit options are a factor, even though he says not to worry about that."

"Well," Lillian said, "also likely will you have visitors. Or maybe you don't want visitors."

Xavier came over and topped up Lillian's drink. She smiled at him.

"Yeah, my mom wants to be there, even though we have promised to take pictures, and barring any complications it will be easier once everyone is back home. My parents, being Virginians, think anything inside DC is too hard to get to and harder to park at. And they will not make use of public transit. So, that is also a factor."

Lillian had lived a life lucky enough that she hadn't ever had to think too hard about where the hospitals in the area were located. Her dad had passed away so quickly that he had never even made it to the hospital. And hospital stays for baby births were short enough, that the friends she knew who had had babies had been home before she could post congrats on their social media announcement.

"I get along pretty well with my mom, but I'm not sure I'd want her in the room for anything that involved me being half naked. Even though I know she'd tell me she'd seen it all before," Lillian said. This was another reason Lillian was glad she wasn't planning to have kids. She was happy for people around her to have kids that she could buy gifts for. But no, no desire to add to the planetary population for herself.

"Yeah, my parents would also drive the medical staff crazy questioning all their choices. So, it is best for everyone for them to see us once we're back home. They will also question all our decisions about living in an apartment, in a city, and likely the kind of diapers we've bought. But they were going to do that anyway."

"Nothing wrong with raising kids in a city or an apartment," Mr. Watkins said. "Multi-family housing helps remind us we're all in a community. Which is a helpful reminder when you are trying to teach kids to consider others."

Lillian hadn't thought about that. Certainly, living in dorms, and now an apartment building had encouraged her to think about things like noise, and smells and having loud parties. But she had grown up in a suburb, but also a house with a sibling, and they all had devices that made noise, and things could get cacophonous fast. "I feel like I should defend the suburbs, but I do see your point."

"Which suburb did you grow up in?" Mr. Watkins asked.

"Silver Spring," she said.

"Were you in a house? And were you still inside the Beltway, or the other side?"

"This is a very thorough line of questioning, Mr. Watkins." Xavier said.

"I don't mind," Lillian said. "House, small though. Ranch style. Inside the Beltway. Though my school wasn't always."

"So, that's similar. Silver Spring isn't quite as big as DC, but it's not what you might call bucolic."

"Well, that's a great scrabble word," Bailey said.

"I do like to play the word games," Mr. Watkins said.

Lillian had played a bunch of word games for a while and then they all started to feel less like fun and more like homework, so she had stopped. Long term commitment was just not her thing.

"Do you have a good book or whatever for the hospital?" Lillian asked.

"I don't know that I'll be able to concentrate on a book. But we've got some good podcast episodes that we've saved up," Bailey said. She had gotten up and was back behind the bar.

"That works," Lillian said. "So basically, you're hoping this hospital is good and you can be done after the tour, is that the goal?"

"Yep," Bailey said. "Then Tomas can finalize his color-coded birth plan, and we can move on to the eat bonbons and wait stage."

"Color-coded. Has he been talking to Louise?"

"No," Bailey said. "In fact, he is not allowed to talk to Louise until after this baby is born."

"I will say nothing," Lillian said smiling. Lillian loved Louise, found her love of list apps adorable. But Louise could be a lot when she went into planning mode. Louise had given her a book, a Patreon suggestion, and a podcast to listen to when Lillian had mentioned her apartment was cluttered. She no longer talked about that around Louise. It was all done with love. But it was a lot.

"You doing okay over here?" Xavier asked.

"I'm good," Lillian said.

"This is a very nice community you've cultivated here," Mr. Watkins said. "I hope you know that."

"Thanks," Xavier said.

"Um," Bailey said. "I'm here because I get paid. No offense."

Xavier smiled. "None taken."

"Still, it's a good group. The neighborhood is lucky to have you."

"Thanks," Xavier said. "We're lucky the neighborhood includes nice people like you too."

Bailey closed out Mr. Watkins' tab and they all waved goodbye to him.

The door shut behind him and Bailey glanced at Xavier. "Suck up," she said.

Lillian giggled.

"Hey," Xavier said. "He owns some of the buildings on this block. He's one of the folks that told the ANC they should give us a chance. Also, he's a customer. Who tips. So, you can call it sucking up. I call it good business."

"You find this cute?" Bailey said to Lillian.

"I kinda do," Lillian said.

Bailey sighed. "Really no accounting for taste here."

Lillian chuckled again.

"She's making fun of both of us," Xavier said.

"I know," Lillian said. "But I have a younger brother. I'm used to being heckled."

# Chapter 19

Xavier loaded up the dishwasher after he and Lillian had scrounged a very late breakfast. She was sipping coffee on the couch.

His phone buzzed.

"Xavier, help," Nani said.

"Hi, Nani, what's the problem?" Xavier asked.

"So, I want to go on this TV show, and my parents are acting like I want to become a stripper. Which, obviously sex work is work, and their reaction would still be inappropriate, but I'm literally going on a TV show about genealogy. But they say I'm being silly, and I should focus on my career. Which, I am. My goal is to be on TV. So, I would like to be on a TV show."

"Yeah, I'm not sure why they would care either," Xavier said. He remembered his mom speculating that people would figure out Nani wasn't in college. But he didn't think that was it. She could be on TV and be in college.

"So, if auntie and uncle ask, I never said anything like this, but do you need their permission to be on the show?"

"I don't," Nani said. "The show had said it was a good idea to let your family know and that they could help answer any questions the family might have. I gave them the show's number, but I don't know if they used it. Wait. I think they did. The researcher said something to me about my parents and if I had talked to them and were they feeling better about things."

"Do they need something like family photos or information from your parents?" Xavier asked.

"Please, all that is on social media. My life has been documented from literally day one. Plus, it's not like it's hard to find our family tree. Oh, I guess they might have asked my parents if they wanted to do DNA testing. I wonder if that's it. My dad has gotten a little sketch about the government tracking all our data. Which like, yes, the

83

surveillance state is bad. But also. Lol. He still uses Facebook. And we know they track all our data."

"Um, Nani," Xavier said. He tried to figure out the gentlest way to say this. He could be wrong of course. But. "Could you parents be worried about the DNA testing?"

"What, you think my parents have extra kids they don't want finding them. Or...oh shit. But it can't be. I look just like everybody."

"You know we're not giving you up no matter what the test says or doesn't say, right?" Xavier said.

"Oh crud. Okay, guess I call to call my parents back. Thanks, Xavier."

"You're welcome. Love you, cuz."

"Well that sounded like a fun conversation," Lillian said.

"I hope I'm wrong and she'll call me back and tell me I'm a paranoid weirdo."

"Well, you are kind of a weirdo. But she probably would have gotten there eventually. But parent stuff is always a little weird."

"Yeah. I can't tell if I should warn my mom or hope she never finds out about it."

"Will your mom be able to do anything useful if she has a heads up now?"

"No," Xavier said. "Like she's a great person and all that. But she would call her sister and ask her are you worried about the DNA test. And well, Nani is probably going to know to lead up to the question with a little more subtlety. But my mom will be pissed I didn't tell her."

"So your choice is your mom being pissed, or your aunt and maybe your uncle and cousin being pissed. The numbers do seem to be on the side of quiet."

"Yeah." Xavier still felt itchy about. Secrets never really stayed secret.

# Chapter 20

"So," Lillian said as they walked home from the bar, "you and Zane had a place and then pandemic, etc. So would you open another place?" She didn't think it was the sex haze making her think he should expand, although sex haze could not be discounted. But she had watched Xavier on nights he worked. His staff loved him. He was on top of things, but not rigid. More owners should be like him. Less shouty farty guys, please.

"Maybe. The timing wasn't right for what we planned. And a lot of the new things that seem to be doing well right now aren't my thing. Like tiki, which as a Hawaiian, absolutely not, or speakeasy, which is really just inconvenient and overpriced. Not my jam."

"Oh, that reminds me, why does your bar have an apostrophe in the name?"

"Did Zane put you up to this?" Xavier asked as he opened the door to his condo.

"No, should I ask him?" Lillian pulled out her phone. She was absolutely not going to text her brother in the middle of the night about a bar her brother wasn't even supposed to know she knew about. But always gotta make the threat believable.

"No, I'll tell you. I was going for 'Bottoms Up' like the thing you say before you drink, like 'Cheers' or 'Slainte'."

"Things people say when they are drinking. Yes, I get you."

"Right, so I submitted it to the sign person, who - well there have been many theories, but basically, she decided I meant to have an apostrophe there. Maybe she thought it was a name, or had somehow never heard the phrase 'bottoms up'. The sign arrived. I saw the apostrophe. Pulled out the paperwork. Called them up, and she was like yes, I fixed it for you and didn't even charge you for the apostrophe. And now I'm realizing to redo this sign will take time, and even if I'm right, which I was, who cares. It was clear enough."

"Aw, you didn't want to hurt the nice lady's feelings." Lillian was not a puddle. Or not that kind of puddle, over this story.

"I mean probably I should have told her so she would stop fixing," he made air quotes," other people's signs."

"You're so sweet," Lillian said. "I need water." She dumped her stuff and got a big glass of water. It was Friday, well, technically already Saturday now so neither of them needed to get up early tomorrow. But she needed to hydrate. "Okay, like don't take this the wrong way," Lillian said.

"Things people say before saying something offensive for $100, Alex," Xavier said.

"You know Alex is dead, right?"

"You know most people don't know who the current host is, but they know Alex, right?"

"Fair point." Lillian shrugged. "Anyway. I like your weirdly named bar. But there are people who want more of an experience. And if they are willing to pay for that, why not?

"I'm not saying they can't have that. But my interest is not in the kitschy or the fake illegal experience."

"Okay, so what would you do if money was no object?"

"Money is always an object."

"Okay, I recognize you are not in a brainstorming mood. So just think about it. You dreamed up a whole thing with Zane once. I know your ideas in there." She finished her glass of water. "Are we done with the talking portion of the evening?"

"It's not really evening," Xavier said.

Lillian knew one way to make him stop talking.

# Chapter 21

Xavier was trying to figure out orders for February. They did a banner business in February. The restaurant workers that made up the bulk of their clientele were run ragged with the Superbowl, and then Valentine's Day. They worked long hours and had even more steam to blow off after. Plus, the darkness always seemed to really start getting to people in February.

Whereas March it started to feel like spring and things slowed down a little. At least until spring break started. Alcohol didn't go bad, so it wasn't the end of the world if they had too much stock. But it cost money, and took space to store, and so, even with the supply chain issues that were the norm these days, he had to find a balance.

Maybe by March he'd have time to talk to Lillian about whatever they were doing. It was going great, so he hadn't wanted to mess with it, but they needed to define it or something. Xavier was so out of practice with this. But communication was key to avoiding misunderstandings. So, they needed to communicate about more than sex and food.

"Hey, boss?" Della said standing in the doorway.

"Hey, what's up?" he said. "You're not on yet, right?" Xavier looked at the clock on the laptop. He usually was pretty good about not zoning out on spreadsheets and missing the start of shift. Two Bars had started closing on Wednesdays, so Della had been added to the Wednesday rotation.

"So, I know we talked about keeping me part time until Bailey goes on leave, but Vance is closing Two Bars at the end of the month. So, I'm going to be more available for whatever."

"Vance is closing Two Bars? Is he rebranding?"

Della shrugged. "I'm not sure. He's also closing the one by the Wharf too, so he may be consolidating."

Vance's Wharf space was giant, so Xavier was sure the overhead was huge. But Two Bars was a small intimate space, that depending on the lease terms, theoretically would need to sell a few drinks a night to cover the cost of staff. Especially when you cheaped out and only staffed one person at a time. If Vance was getting out of all things, then it would make sense to get rid of Two Bars too. But if Vance was keeping his other location open, then he was a fool for not snapping Della up to work at it. But Vance's foolishness was Xavier's gain.

"Well, let me look at the schedule, but I definitely think we can find more shifts for you. We've loved having you. And I know I sound weird when I say we like that, but I did ask the others and they all had raves."

"Well, that's nice to hear. The late hours have been an adjustment, but it's a good team. And I like being busy, so it's good."

"Good. I'll text y'all after I rejigger the schedule."

"Cool."

Xavier finalized the orders. And then he scrolled through his contacts to find his buddy who used to work at Vance's original bar.

Xavier: Hey, I heard Vance is closing a few places?

Claude: Really? My spies have failed me. Lemme reach out.

Claude liked referring to everyone as spies.

Xavier looked up the leaseholder for Two Bars. Lanny Watkins. Huh. Lanny was a regular at Bottom's Up. He liked to give Xavier crap about his apostrophe in the sign.

Claude: Oh, this story needs to be told in person. You at the bar tonight?

Xavier: Yep.

Claude: I'll bring champagne.

Xavier: You can bring whatever you want. That's not what we serve here. Drink your champagne somewhere else.

Claude: Charge me corkage.

Xavier: Or I could just kick you out.

Claude: Party pooper. Fine. I'll save the champagne for people who appreciate it.

Xavier: [thumbs up emoji]

The night started slow. Xavier had his laptop out at the far end of the bar, working on updating the schedule. He could give Della some shifts he had planned to cover himself. He'd check with Bailey too. She was close to delivering and he knew she was having issues standing. They had put in a stool for her. But there was so much moving back and forth between pouring drafts, and taking the glasses back and forth. The amount of time you could spend on the stool during any given shift wasn't too long.

Dan was getting close with his food truck, so might want to cut back also.

No sign of Claude, but knowing him he really had stopped to drink a bottle of champagne.

"Mr. Watkins," he said when Lanny walked in.

"Now, none of that, unless you want me to start calling you Mr. Xavier."

"It has a certain ring to it. Have you met Della?"

"Hello, Ms. Della," Lanny said. "Didn't you used to work at Two Bars?"

"Still do," Della said. "For now, at least."

"Did I hear you own the building Two Bars is in?" Xavier asked.

"As a matter of fact, I do," Lanny said.

"So is Vance giving up the lease, if you're comfortable sharing that?" Xavier asked.

"Oh, I think it's okay for me to tell you my renter has informed me he will be breaking the lease. I have to tell you, I hadn't been sure I wanted to have a bar in that building. The ANC is kind of particular, and I had sort of envisioned something that was open more during the daytime. But I looked at how this space here was providing such a nice community spot, and being kind of an anchor in the neighborhood and I thought, well, Lanny, let's give it a shot."

DC had Advisory Neighborhood Commissions, or ANCs, that weighed in on things like liquor licenses and zoning for their area.

Claude walked in and sat down next to Lanny. Claude looked at Xavier. "Are you ready? Wait." He looked at Della. "You are new. Hello, I am Claude. You must tell me everything about you."

Xavier shook his head. "Della, this is Claude. He used to work at Rock and Squirrel."

"Hello," Della said. "Boss, I gotta tell you, I haven't seen you be this social, well, like ever. Is it your birthday?"

Claude laughed. "Oh, I like you."

"Well, Xavier, if you have any ideas what I can do with that space, you certainly should not hesitate to let me know." Lanny placed cash on the bar and saluted everyone before walking out.

"Are you going to open another spot?" Claude asked.

"No," Xavier said. Though he thought of Lillian asking him that just recently. It was like she knew. But it wasn't the right time or place. Even if knowing the landlord wasn't a jerk was a plus. The logical side of his brain kept saying, well, your last new idea didn't work. People always wanted to spout platitudes, like half the restaurants fail, and the pandemic hit the industry hard. It was all true. But if half the restaurants and bars failed, and he had one success and one failure, a third one seemed like asking for more failure. "Lanny owns the building Two Bars is in, so I was asking him what happened with the lease."

"You should take it over."

"And do what with it?" Xavier asked. "Besides, aren't you here to tell us what you learned from your spies."

"Fine," Claude said. "Be that way. Okay, here's the scoop. Remember how Vance was up in Connecticut because he married a lovely human who lives in Connecticut and they wanted to spend more time together?'

Xavier nodded.

"Well, apparently he had, in typical Vance fashion also found a hot young thing to hook up with. To be clear, Vance's wife is both hot and young. Vance is just into quantity. Anyhoodle, hot young thing was apparently also hooking up with the wife, and confronted them both, and now they are getting a divorce. Rumor has it the wife wants half the restaurants, and so he's making the half smaller."

"Doesn't that make his half smaller also?" Della asked.

"It does, but like don't tell him. Also, he's probably stashed something somewhere until after the divorce. Vance looks after Vance."

"He seemed to, ah well, it doesn't matter," Xavier said. Xavier was in no place to talk about secret relationships. Although his wasn't a secret to anyone he was sleeping with. "So, Rock and Squirrel he kept?"

"Yeah, he got a really good long-term lease on Rock and Squirrel because he moved in when they were still rebuilding the hotel. If he closed, the landlord would easily triple the rent."

"That's also gonna happen at the Wharf, but I guess that's a risk he's willing to take. Wait, didn't he have one more spot. A high end one or something?"

Claude frowned.

"Orange Rose," Della said. "It was where I first started. There was some sort of issue with one of the liquor distributors. And he ended up closing temporarily. Or it was supposed to be temporary. But that was a year ago."

"Do you remember the name of the liquor distributor?" Claude asked.

Della made a face. "I never met them. Vance handled that."

Xavier shook his head. That probably meant the distributor was hot. Vance was hardly in town these days, it would make sense to have one of the on-site people handle the ordering so that if there were issues, someone on site would know. "Wait. It would have to be either Grand Liquor or Tequila Etc. There aren't that many that will actually deliver in DC."

"Grand Liquor's rep is Stevie," Claude said. "She's like forty though. Not Vance's usual demographic."

"Tequila Etc. I thought was Joe," Xavier said. Bottom's Up worked with Grand Liquor and two local brands that he bought from directly. But at Schism they had worked with Tequila Etc. "But he was training someone new."

"Who do we know who uses Tequila Etc.?" Claude asked.

Xavier was pretty sure he shouldn't encourage Claude. Except Xavier loved a puzzle. He made spreadsheets for fun. Okay, they were for work. But yeah, he loved getting everything to line up.

"Phan," Xavier said.

"Oh, of course. I'm texting him right now."

"Okay, I knew you all knew a lot of people," Della said, "but this is hilarious. Six degrees of bartenders."

"It had to be like this in Philly too," Xavier said.

"It was. That's part of why I left."

"Ooh, I sense a story," Claude said. "Want to share?"

Xavier scanned the bar. It was still light enough, and Wednesday enough that they just had a few other customers who were slowly nursing their drinks. In another hour, they'd get the first wave of folks getting off shift at the family restaurants that closed early. Wednesdays it tended to be gentle waves. Not the packed madness that happened Friday through Sunday.

"It's not that great a story," Della said. "Hooked up with someone for a bit. She wanted to be exclusive. I was less into that. She didn't take it well. People took sides. Yada yada."

"That sucks," Xavier said. "It's not really a bright side, but we're glad to have you here."

"Xavier, you are like the sappiest," Claude said.

"That's not even the first time today, he told me that."

"You should write a study, on positive reinforcement in the restaurant industry."

"Because so many bar owners read studies," Xavier said. He had realized pretty quickly that running a bar meant staff, and staff meant managing, and he should probably learn about managing people. He'd certainly had good and bad managers, and even one who was nice but ineffectual when things actually needed to change. But there was a difference between knowing all the things you should not do and knowing how to be good. But providing regular feedback so people knew if they were doing well was an easy one.

"They should read studies. You should be the one who owns all the places, not Vance," Claude said.

"Maybe I should marry Vance next," Xavier said. Though blustery and loud had never been his type.

Claude and Della both cracked up laughing and they moved on to other subjects. The crowd started to pick up and Xavier and Della were both filling orders and starting and closing tabs. But Xavier kept thinking about being Vance.

He didn't really want to be Vance. But maybe he missed the challenge of serving other kinds of clientele. He loved the Bottom's Up customer base. It was a rare bar or restaurant concept that appealed to the entire swath of the population. Having a customer target was sensible market planning. But sometimes he would have a great idea for something and it would be great for a different kind of place. Something more family friendly, or in the other direction, something for the fancier crowd. Not a speakeasy, but something that pulled the people who went to speakeasies. Sometimes, if he knew someone with the right kind of place he would text them the idea. But a lot of them weren't for just any place.

Of course, bright ideas were all well and good but they were a small part of what these places needed. Not everyone had enough money to be able to afford to close some of their business in order to appear less rich. Some people were operating on a different scale.

# Chapter 22

"Lillian," her mom said, her voice tinny on the phone, like it was on speaker phone, are you bringing anyone with you for Chinese New Year?"

"Just me," she said. Her mom had not mentioned Lillian dating since Thanksgiving, so Lillian had thought maybe that was a phase. But apparently no. "Are you bringing anyone, or I guess inviting anyone? It's a big year for you."

It was the year of her mom's animal. There were a lot of theories about that being sometimes bad luck. But Lillian chose to believe differently. A year about you was great. And sure, being more you, meant more good traits and more flaws. But mostly a you year had to be awesome. And the last year it had been her year being the year she was dating the identity stealing ex, like obviously he agreed, because he wanted to be her. Yes. Yes, that was it.

"Who would I invite?" her mom said. "But if you don't want to date Xavier, you should ask Zane and Louise if they know other people."

"I will do that," Lillian said. Because asking them if they knew other people was easy. And yes, she knew what her mom really meant. But maybe once her mom's big year started, she'd come up with something else to focus on.

Lillian could suggest knitting, but she suspected once her mom found out how much yarn cost, she'd hate it. Also, her mom and the knitting ladies? They would not stop trying to couple her up.

"Maybe you should join a book club, Mom." Her mom still met up with some of the other parents from when Lillian and Zane were in Chinese school. But she suspected all they talked about was their kids' marriages and babies. Maybe some friends who talked about something else would be good.

"They read boring stuff," her mom said.

"Oh, there's some good ones. There's one where they read cozy mysteries and drink wine."
"Is it just for young people?"
"I'll send you the info. We can check it out."
"Okay. Do you think you might find someone at the book club?" He mother asked.

Well, so much for distraction. "We can certainly see." Lillian could, of course, tell her mom she was dating Xavier. But her mom would tell Zane. And also, Lillian was kind of enjoying the separation. It wasn't like she was hiding Xavier because they didn't like Xavier. But a theoretical boyfriend was different than a real one. Besides, Xavier wasn't even really a boyfriend. It was less relationship more situationship. Basically, she showed up at either the bar, or his place, when their schedules aligned and they had sex.

It was all the good stuff, none of the arguing over dishes. Okay, sometimes they got takeout and there were dishes. And she had logged into her streaming account on his TV, and now just watched that one show over at his place.

But it is not like they went out together. Had dates. Of course, Xavier's work schedule was a lot. But Lillian liked things as they were. She had plenty of friends if there was a movie or play she wanted to see while Xavier was working.

Things were great. As much as Lillian loved her family, they didn't need to know.

# Chapter 23

Xavier sat up in bed. He realized how to fix the schedule. He got up and threw on some boxers because he liked to have his bits covered before he sat in front of a device with a camera.

He sat down at the desk and popped open the laptop and swapped two names, and yep, everything popped green. Thank goodness. He'd send the email after coffee.

Lillian walked in from the bedroom and went straight to the coffee maker. She popped a coffee pod in then turned to look at him. "You got out of bed on a Saturday to work?"

Xavier paused. Okay, yes, he could see how that looked. "Sorry, I was trying to figure out a puzzle with the schedule and when I woke up, I had the answer. I do need to send it out, but that can wait until after breakfast."

"Okay," Lillian said. "Do you often wake up with answers, because that seems amazing."

"Not that often. But sometimes if I'm trying to solve something, going to sleep helps. I'm never sure if it's the rest, the processing time or both."

"Wow, if I'm trying to figure something out before bed, I often just can't sleep. It's like the problem-solving part of me won't shut off. So, I try not to think about problems before sleep."

"That seems hard." Xavier had always been good at sleeping when he needed to. It made the late-night schedule much more bearable.

"Sex helps. Especially good sex. Clears away all the thoughts."

"I could see that," Xavier said carefully.

"Why don't you send your email now and then we can hop back into bed."

"Okay." Xavier tried to think about boring staid things while he crafted and sent the email and then sent the text to the employee chat to look out for it.

"Can I ask a very random question?" Lillian said. She put her empty coffee cup on the counter.

""Sure." Xavier closed the laptop and stood up carefully.

"Why do you like briefs over boxer briefs?"

"Boxer briefs are just overly long briefs. I don't need briefs that support my thighs."

"Makes sense. Shall we put them away for now?"

"Yeah."

They did not get back out of bed for a while.

*** 

By mid-afternoon, Lillian and Xavier had put on clothes and moved to the couch so they could watch a movie.

"Oh," Lillian said, "I have Chinese New Year stuff Friday, so I'll be at my mom's til after midnight. I'll probably crash at home after. But Saturday I am all yours. Or like I will show up at the bar and then we can do whatever."

"Am I supposed to get you like a red envelope?" Xavier asked.

"You are not my elder so no," Lillian said. "Wait, are you my elder? Let me see your license?"

"You could just ask me. You don't need to see my license."

"Well, now I want to know why you won't show me your license." Lillian knew she was being ridiculous. He should be protective of his license. His data. And yet, she wanted it. Now. For some reason.

"I will show it to you, I was just pointing out that you could ask me." Xavier reached for his wallet and handed her the license.

Lillian examined it. "How is your picture so good?" He honestly looked so much like himself in the license photo. So many people herself included looked like flat deer-in the-headlights versions of themselves. Not good. Xavier looked like himself, steady, and normal, like taking pics at the DMV was just a normal thing he did.

She looked at his birth year and pulled out her phone to figure out what animal that made him in the Chinese zodiac. "Oh my god, of course you are," she said. "You're an ox."

"Oh yeah, I knew that."

The ox was also rumored to be very compatible with the snake, which she was, but that was all just silliness. Silliness was little unfair. Lillian knew plenty of people who lived up to the traits that their animal was supposed to be, more than could be explained by coincidence or people just being types. But also, you couldn't let the things people said about it all rule all the decisions you made. Like if the prediction said you would make a lot of money, you still had to do all the work to make money. Also, her prediction almost never said she was going to make a lot of money, which was a shame.

"So, do you guys have like special foods you eat, or things you do for the holiday?" Xavier said. "I ask because my mom keeps discovering Hawaiian traditions and then like telling me about them."

"You didn't do a lot of Hawaiian stuff growing up.?"

"We did like some stuff. Like I had books with Hawaiian kids stories. And like we talked about stuff that was going on in Hawai'i, and of course we'd visit some. But when people are like what's all the Hawaiian stuff you did, I'm mostly like, I dunno, we just were - are, Hawaiian."

"I mean that's fair. Did your parents grow up in Hawai'i?"

"They did. They met in college here, and stayed. Well, until they didn't."

"So, like a lot of it was normal stuff to them. It's not exactly the same. But, no, never mind."

"Tell me," Xavier said.

"Well, so with first generation immigrants, they move to a new country, and like all these things are different. Their kids grow up with all these back in China or whatever stories. Their connection is to stuff that is tied to a specific point in time. But like obviously, Hawai'i is part of the US, so like you don't have to decide to uproot your whole life, you don't have to apply for a visa or anything. You just get to hop a place or boat and move. But your parents wouldn't have the same sense of - like you're so lucky you get to grow up on the East Coast. So they wouldn't necessarily have worked to make sure you felt connected to everything."

"Hmm, yeah. Could be." Xavier rubbed her shoulder. "And maybe my mom sort of wishes she had now. So, she's like trying to teach me after the fact."

"Could be."

"Anyway, I'm actually not on the schedule Friday, " Xavier said. "Della needs more shifts because Two Bars is shutting down."

"Aw, I loved Two Bars. But are you going to have enough work for Della. Even if you're not on the schedule, I know you're going to check in."

"Yeah, Bailey's going to be on maternity leave soon. Dan's working on stuff for his food truck launch. Unika moved to part time, because she's in grad school. I probably need another person. But not full time, which is tough to find."

Lillian wondered if she should ask Xavier if he wanted to be dragooned into coming to Chinese New Year. Lillian knew if she mentioned it to Zane, he would do it. But Lillian didn't want to have to have him and her family in the same room. It would somehow feel too dishonest.

"Are you going to know what to do with yourself with a free night?"

"Yeah. I'll be fine."

"To be clear, I mean will you know what to do that is not going to the bar and checking on things?"

"I mean, I am going to check on them. That's just being a good manager. But I will watch TV, catch up on admin. Stuff like that."

"Oh wow, I know you said you were a workaholic. But I think I am going to have to teach you how to relax or whatever."

"I'm not learning to knit. Not because of toxic masculinity, but more because crafts are not my jam. Unless, are puzzles a craft?"

"Making them or putting them together?"

"Putting them together."

"Do you have a secret puzzle stash?" Lillian thought she had poked in all the corners of his apartment. Had she overlooked a batch of puzzles?

"No, I do not."

"Okay, there's a puzzle store right next to the bookstore. We can go tomorrow and get you some."

"Okay," Xavier said.

Lillian nodded and then settled back as they started the movie. Xavier was less a puzzle and more like a kaleidoscope. Every time she thought she had him figured out, he'd shift and reveal a little more.

# Chapter 24

"Happy almost you year, Mom! I brought ice cream. And sorbet," Lillian said. She toed off her shoes and hefted the freezer bag into the kitchen and popped open the freezer. "Mom, there's like no room in here."

"I didn't know I needed to clean the freezer for you. I like to have things in case there are unexpected guests."

"When was the last time there were unexpected guests?" Lillian asked.

"Thanksgiving."

Lillian refrained from pointing out they had used zero of that food for Thanksgiving. "Well, let me put find space for these and we'll just have to eat lots."

She had to take the pints out of the freezer bag, so she could stuff them into what little space was left. She had only gotten four pints. But she figured whatever was leftover, she would take home.

"Why did you bring ice cream?"

"And sorbet. I told you I was bringing dessert."

"I thought it would be pie."

"These are Lunar New Year flavors."

"How is ice cream lunar New Year flavored? Is it soy sauce?"

Lillian refrained from mention she had actually once had an amazing soy sauce sorbet. There was a lot of refraining today. "There's almond cookie, barley tea, black sesame, and pandan."

"There's pandan ice cream?"

"That one is a sorbet."

Her mom nodded.

She followed her mom into the dining room. The table had bamboo baskets of dumplings, rice, steamed chicken, peanut noodles, and salad. "This looks great, Mom."

Growing up the Chinese school had always done a Chinese New Year celebration for the families, so they had always gone to eat there. Lillian had learned to make dumplings, but at school not at home. But this year, her mom had said she wanted to cook for them, instead of ordering in. And since she had let them order for Thanksgiving, Lillian and Zane had both agreed to this. Her mom didn't seem tired, or stressed the way the Thanksgiving cooking had always seemed to make her. So maybe this was fine.

It was weird to reach the age where you worried about your parent as much as they probably worried about you. Lillian's mom wasn't very old or anything. But Lillian was more aware of how much time and energy simple household chores took, that the repetitive need to regularly feed yourself could take a toll. And of course, her dad hadn't been that old either. But she was mostly over worrying that her mom could keel over at any moment.

And Lillian had never, well, almost never had a bad dumpling. Something about wrapping food in dough that really just made it delightful. So, if they had ordered in, let someone else do the work, that would have been great. But if it made her mom happy to cook this for them, then that was great too.

"Hello!" Zane called out. "We're here to eat."

"I mean, we are also here to see your family who you love," Louise said.

"That goes without saying," Zane said.

"Uh huh," Louise said.

"Let's all sit and eat before the food gets cold. Also, Lillian brought too much dessert and it will melt."

"Ooh, you got the ice cream?" Louise asked.

"I did indeed," Lillian said.

"Yum. Also, this all looks so great, Mrs. Yang," Louise said.

"Marian," her mom said.

"Marian," Louise said.

They passed around plates and chopsticks, and everyone piled food onto their plates.

"This is so good, Mom," Zane said. "You're going to have to give me the dumpling recipe."

"It's just a basic one, it's not special."

"Well, then it won't take long for you to give it to me," Zane said.

Her mom nodded and Lillian could tell she was pleased. Lillian loved eating dumplings more than she liked making them. So, she was grateful there were people who made really good frozen ones that she could stock in her freezer and make in batches of like six, or twelve, depending on how hungry she was feeling. Sometimes she put then on top of a salad and then it was like an entire entree. An entire delicious entree. She should take some over to Xavier's freezer. His freezer was pretty bare.

Lillian's phone buzzed and she pulled it out and tried to check it surreptitiously under the table. Her mom didn't usually get super strict about phones at the dinner table, but she'd ask who it was. And since it was Xavier, then it would be weird.

Lillian liked being in a secret situationship. She liked not having to explain to Zane that she was an adult who could do what or whom she wanted. She liked not explaining to her mom that a situationship wasn't leading to marriage or kids, it was about the now and that was exactly the way she liked it. But also, it was one thing to not tell her family. Actively lying felt like a different level.

Xavier: Bailey had her baby. Zetta Jane. Happy, healthy, all that stuff.

Lillian: Yay! Do we need to set up like a meal train or something?

Xavier: What is a meal train? Is that like an app?

Lillian looked up and everyone was focused on their food, but if she kept texting, they were going to notice.

Lillian: We'll talk later.

She put her phone in her pocket so she wouldn't be tempted to respond again. She felt it buzz again two more times. It was so tempting to check, but no. She grabbed a piece of chicken and stuffed it in her mouth.

Her phone buzzed in her pocket again. Xavier was not usually this much of a texter. He always remembered all the stuff she'd told him in the text, so he was reading everything. But texting was more informational for him. Less conversational.

She saw Louise giving her a considering look and adopted her most, I'm just here for the food expression. Zane's phone buzzed and he pulled it put and put it right on the table and looked at it.

Lillian had at least tried to be subtle.

"Oh, wow, Bailey had her baby. She works at Xavier's bar," Zane said to their mom.

"Xavier had a baby?" Mom asked.

"No, Bailey, one of his employees had a baby. The baby is not his."

"Oh, okay," Mom said. "Well, good."

"We should send them like a food delivery gift card," Louise said.

Oh, a food delivery gift card probably made more sense. Lillian had no idea how many of Xavier's employees cooked. Dan did. He was probably already planning to drop off soup. But if everyone got them gift cards for the same delivery service, then they could make a bunch of orders. Also, if Dan stocked them up with so much soup, they didn't need anything for a while, the gift cards wouldn't go bad in the fridge. Lillian remembered after her dad died, people had sent them so much food. It had been great, and sweet, and kind. And it turned out they really weren't thinking about eating, so it became a Jenga game, trying to get everything stacked in the fridge.

Ooh, Lillian wondered if Xavier liked Jenga. She should ask him. Later. Not here.

"Do we know what hospital, they are at?" Louise asked. "We could send it there. Otherwise, we could give it to Xavier to give to her. Unless you have her home address."

"I don't have her home address," Zane said. "But I think she's at Georgetown?"

Lillian kept her face incredibly still because she wanted to shake her head. Bailey was at Sibley, not Georgetown. But Lillian could not think of any way to explain how she knew that.

"Xavier would know, right?" Louise asked.

Zane tapped on his phone.

Lillian looked over to see if Mom was getting annoyed at all this table phone use, but she was twirling her noodles, unbothered.

Lillian's phone buzzed in her pocket again. She should gave worn a dress without pockets. The she'd have stuck her phone somewhere else.

Okay, Lillian reminded herself, she was not in charge of people knowing things. Not even her sibling. These were adults who could figure out how to get the answers they needed, and if it took until tomorrow for them to get the correct answer, they would all be fine. Because explaining when and how she had talked to Bailey, explaining when and how she had become a regular at Bottom's Up, did she want to do that here? Now? No, she did not.

"Well, it's good that someone wants to have babies," her mom said.

And yep, that was why. Thanks, universe, for that timely reminder.

Lillian and Louise looked at each other, a sort of do you want to take this, or shall I kind of look. Zane was staring very intently at his phone, like there was very serious news there that required all of his attention.

Lillian smiled and looked at her mom. "I think there are still people who want to have babies, yes."

"I read an article that there are not enough babies being born," Mom said.

"Enough for what?" Lillian asked adopting a neutral tone.

"Babies are so cute," Mom said.

"They are," Lillian said.

"Expensive too," Louise said.

"Oh, you kids always think things you don't want to do are expensive. Things were never cheap. But people figure it out," Mom said.

Lillian was torn. Things were objectively more expensive now. They could certainly talk about that. Lots of baby or kid-centric things were more expensive in the years since Zane and Lillian and Louise had been kids. Daycare cost more, the Chinese school that Zane and Lillian had gone to cost more, to say nothing of rent, food, and all the normal things.

But the reason Lillian didn't currently have kids wasn't because they were expensive, though they were. She didn't have kids for the same reason she had a situationship. She liked being able to blow a ton of money of yarn and not worry about it. She liked being able to say sure, and go to a concert or a show, when someone turned out to have an extra ticket. She liked being able to take a mental health day, rent a car, and go to the beach.

Some of those things were possible with a kid, but they required more complex logistics. Lillian had run out of clean underwear last week and had to buy more because she realized this after the laundry room in her building was closed for the evening. Also, it seemed like people should have kids because they want to. Not because everyone else kept telling them that was the next step on the adulthood ladder. But is that how they wanted to start this new year? Maybe not.

"Are we ready to try that ice cream Lillian brought?" Louise asked.

"Oh, let's go grab that," Lillian said.

Lillian and Louise both got up from the table leaving Zane there.

"Nice distraction," Lillian said softly because her mom had mom ears and could sense a child talking about her in another room.

"Well, I do like ice cream. But yeah, my parents have both told me that I need to wait two more promotions before I can consider kids, which is a whole different kind of pressure."

"Yikes," Lillian said. "So, would it help if they told my mom that?"

"No, because I definitely don't need them creating a whole plan for Zane and I together."

"Ah, so it's good that they don't talk too much then."

"It seems best. Like not keeping them apart per se, more just not insisting they intermingle."

"Got it." Lillian grabbed enough spoons so they could have one per pint. Spoons for eating the ice cream were already on the table. And of course, that's what Lillian was doing. She wasn't keeping her relationship with Xavier a secret so they couldn't get to know him. Zane knew him quite well. She just wasn't encouraging anyone to spend time thinking about them together. A useful separation.

# Chapter 25

"It's my mom," Xavier said, clicking answer on his phone. "Hi, Mom."

Lillian paused the movie they were watching.

"Xavier, why am I the last to know about this?" his mom said.

"Not sure what we're talking about, Mom," Xavier said. Vague seemed the best choice. Listing the things his mother did not know, well, that was a trap that never ended well, that was for sure. He glanced at Lillian. He hadn't talked to his family about her, since they were still on the secret deal that Xavier kept meaning to talk more with Lillian about. But he wanted to not have to watch himself at the bar and with friends.

He was not working to introduce his parents to Lillian. He wasn't embarrassed about her. No, it was more there was no way to introduce her to his parents together since they refused to be in the same room. And there was no way to introduce her to them separately and not have someone get mad they had gotten introduced second.

"My sister tells me that you told your cousin that she was adopted," Mom said.

Oh that. He needed to text Nani. Apparently, she had had the talk with her parents.

"So," he said, knowing that actual truth was useless, but determined to at least try, "I did not know that Nani was adopted. I just told her to talk to Auntie and Uncle about why they didn't want her on the show. Which, I guess, it sounds like she did."

"She did. And now I had to find out on social media, on social media, of all things, that my niece is adopted."

Lillian tapped Xavier's knee and mimed drinking. He shook his head at her. He'd hydrate after the call. She slid away and grabbed her glass to refill it. He missed having her pressed up against him.

"On social media!" Mom repeated.

Xavier was curious what social media this had been announced on, but figured that asking would just make his mom repeat on social media. Maybe he did need water, he was losing focus here.

"That must have been quite a surprise. But I'm glad Nani, and Auntie, and Uncle were comfortable sharing that. That must have been an emotional conversation."

"I know you kids all love putting your stuff on the internet. But it used to be you would tell the family these things in person."

Xavier refrained from mentioning his parents had called him when he was in college to announce their divorce. Separately. "Hmm," he said as neutrally as possible.

"Well, Xavier, I understand this is not a shock to you, because you had time to prepare, but I did not have that information because my son did not share it with me."

Xavier had taken a dealing with difficult customers seminar at some point. They mentioned that often customers got emotional and couldn't be emotional about the thing they wanted to be emotional about, so took it out on a service worker, because sadly that was often considered acceptable, in their minds. Xavier was a son here, and not a service worker. But it did seem his mom might be mad that her sister hadn't told her this news before she told everyone. Or everyone who followed her on social media.

But his mom probably understood that she couldn't yell at her sister for not telling her a thing and not seem like she was stomping on Nani, Auntie, and Uncle's joyous announcement. So, his mom was redirecting at him.

It helped a little to have figured out the plausible explanation, so he didn't accidentally say, "Yell at your sister and not me. Except don't yell at her. This was obviously hard for her."

He settled on, "Mom, I'm sorry you feel like you were left out. I just told Nani to talk to Auntie and Uncle. I did not know what they would tell her. So I didn't have anything to tell you."

"Well, does your father know?"

"I have no idea, Mom. I heard it from you," Xavier said.

"You should tell him."

"Okay, I will do that," Xavier said.

"Any other conversations you have suggested your cousins have recently?" Mom asked.

"No," Xavier said.

"Well, I guess that's something. Don't forget to tell your father," Mom said.

"I won't."

Lillian held up her glass. "Do you need water or something stronger after all that."

"Water is good," Xavier said leaning back on the couch.

He texted his dad.

Xavier: Don't know if you heard, but Uncle and Auntie and Nani announced that she is adopted.

He waited a bit, but not sign that his dad had read it. His dad would see it eventually.

"Did your mom yell at you?" Lillian asked placing the water in front of him and sliding a hand along his shoulder.

"She is very upset that she found out from social media."

"Parents get a little weird about that. But everyone announces babies and weddings that way."

"They do? Am I missing babies and weddings not being on social media?"

"Basically yes. Though you know about Bailey."

"True. Is anyone else I know announcing news on social media?"

"There is no way I can answer that for you," Lillian said.

"We're not on social media, right?" Xavier said.

"I'm on social media, but if you mean I have made us social media official, then no. That would sort of be the opposite of keeping things under wraps."

"We're still doing the secret thing?" Xavier said even though he knew the answer. Lillian always distracted him with sex when he asked, and well, he had gotten to kind of like that. They didn't need an excuse to have sex. But he liked sex with Lillian. So, not much downside really.

And sure enough she leaned in to kiss him instead of answering. Pretty soon he forgot the question.

# Chapter 26

"So, I need to drop something at your place, can I borrow your key?" Lillian asked.

"Can I ask what it is?" Xavier said. "I mean yes, you can have my key, but I am curious. Unless..."

He gave her a look that curled a little something inside her.

"It's puzzles," Lillian said, holding up the tote.

"Puzzles?" Xavier pulled out his key chain, and unhooked one of the keys and handed it over.

"Yep, I'll be back momentarily." Lillian took the puzzles back and tried to quell the flutter nervous feeling in her stomach. It wasn't a big deal. He would either like the puzzles or not. They had been free. She took a deep breath in after depositing them on the coffee table and then went back to Bottom's Up.

"You bought puzzles?" Xavier slid a drink to her.

Lillian sat and sipped. "Thanks. And no, I did not buy puzzles. I swapped them. Well, not really because I didn't have any puzzles. But I reached out to the puzzle swap people and they said they often had extras, that everyone had already done. And if I was willing to let everyone else swap first, I could take a few. So I did." They had never managed to make it to the puzzle store. But when she saw the swap, she had figured she could go on his behalf, since their meetup times were all right as the bar was opening.

"There's a puzzle swap?"

"Yep. People buy puzzles and then they finish them and then they want more, but puzzles cost money, and the boxes take up room, so they swap?"

"How did you - you should start a social media account or something with all this info," Xavier said.

"I'm just collating it. Isn't that basically like me plagiarizing all these newsletters?"

"I don't think so. Besides they want people to know about all their events. You're grabbing some of the cool ones and highlighting them. You could always like footnote it or whatever if you wanted."

"Oh my goodness, we do not footnote on social media. We link. Also, you should hire a social media person. Clearly."

"We don't do specials or anything. What are we going to do, post our hours every night?"

"How did you tell people when you reopened after the pandemic closure? I'm going to hate this answer, aren't I?"

"Texted a few folks. They told more. Some people just showed up."

"Well, good for you for developing a loyal fan base. Social media lets people who don't have your phone number find out about your place. In fact, I am going to go google you guys. Okay fine, you have great reviews, and they all describe the vibe perfectly. So fine. But if you ever start another place, please learn about social media or hire someone or both."

"I can hire you and Louise."

"I think Louise and I are actually pretty expensive." Lillian smiled. Mateo was chatting with another customer at the other end of the bar, so she could be a little bold.

"Also, don't think I didn't notice you deflected away from the original idea that you should do something with all this info you collect. The paper used to do a whole guide for that kind of stuff, but I think they stopped. And well, even if they didn't, I don't think people read the paper to figure out what's cool these days."

"Possibly not. Even though we heart local journalism. The execs at work so often want the stodgier things. Like quirky but with seats and staff, and preferable no QR codes. I of course sometimes find cool ones for myself. But it would be fun to maybe put together a list of like ten things and share it. I'll think about it."

"You do that. And so, when you say your rate is expensive, what kind of currency are we talking about?"

Lillian leaned in. "It might be easier just to show you."

"Yeah, hold that thought." Xavier waved to the customer entering.

Lillian pondered newsletters while sipping her drink. She did like connecting people with fun. Maybe some sort of newsletter would let her do that on a bigger scale.

# Chapter 27

"It is I, and some small thing I found on the street or something," Bailey said walking through the door of Bottom's Up.

"Oh yay!" Lillian spun her stool around.

Xavier looked at Mateo. "You can go, I'm happy to admire from here."

"Don't be scared of the baby," Bailey said.

"I'm not scared of the baby," Xavier said. "I know my strengths. And I will talk to it when it is old enough to learn about alcohol."

"I know you know the baby is not an it," Lillian said. "Here, I will take the baby and let you, sit, Bailey." Lillian reached out and took Zetta, carrying her around to the other folks who had gathered to see.

"Oh, we need to take a picture for Zane. He's working at Circle or he'd be here," Xavier said.

"Oh, that's easy, I can do that," Bailey said. "Lillian, just hold her up."

"Oh," Lillian said, "I'm sure he'd rather have a picture with you holding the baby. Here, let's switch and I'll take it so you can send it."

They transferred the baby back, and Lillian used Bailey's phone to take a picture of the two of them.

Xavier watched as Mateo and Lillian, and a few of their regulars cooed over the baby. Maybe the secret thing had run its course. They needed to talk about that. Because it was starting to get weird.

Once they were back at his place, Lillian stripped down to nothing and Xavier's focus became solely on pleasure. It was only after, that he remembered he had wanted to talk to her about things. But, maybe it was kind of like a sports streak. When things were working, it wasn't worth questioning why they were working. That was only an issue when things stopped working. Right now, things were working. And if that included being discreet, then he could live with that.

# Chapter 28

Torrey: Do you want to go to a concert Tuesday?

Lillian looked at her phone. It was Thursday so that was only a few days away. Torrey was not usually this spontaneous, but Lillian was all for developing some good spontaneity.

Lillian: When and where? I know you said Tuesday, but like specifically.

Torrey: It's at the White Squirrel. I have tickets already.

Lillian: Cool. Let me know what I owe you.

Lillian popped open a window on her laptop to see who was playing. She didn't mind going to concerts for bands she barely knew. She found it kind of fun. These days there was so much music everywhere, that trying to decide what to listen to sometimes overwhelmed her. But there were enough live music venues in DC, that she could go and listen to one band, or two since there would be an opener, and get a feel for them.

She told most of her friends if they needed a concert buddy, she was willing to be it. But this was the first time Torrey had taken her up on it.

Bottom's Up was packed that night. Lillian waved goodbye to Xavier well before closing. It wasn't that she couldn't entertain herself, but when they were super packed, Xavier and whoever else was working ended up checking in with her a lot, to make sure she was still okay. It was sweet, but they had other customers who needed attention. She had tried getting Torrey to come out with her some night, so she had someone to chat with once it got busy. But Torrey said it wasn't her scene.

Walking out of the bar Lillian ran smack dab into Cady. Cady who managed at Circle where her brother worked.

"Oh hey, Cady! It's so great to see you. I don't usually drink here. And now I'm just heading home. But we should hang out some time. At Circle probably."

"Hi, Lillian." Cady put a hand on one hip. "So, you think I'm as clueless as your brother?"

That was a trick question. Lillian smiled winningly, innocently, like a person who did not know where this conversation was headed.

"Look, if you don't want your brother, or anyone to know, that's fine with me. Y'all are consenting adults. But if you actually wanted to keep it secret, maybe you all should not make goo-goo eyes at each other in front of half the industry."

"We do not make goo-goo eyes at each other," Lillian said.

"Uh-huh. Well, I'm gonna go in. If you want, I'm happy to text you when Zane tells me he's headed here. If that is a thing that would be useful."

"Um, yeah, that would be incredibly useful. But I don't want to get you in trouble with Zane."

"Please, he doesn't scare me."

"He doesn't scare me." Lillian felt the need to clarify. "He went a little retro toxic masculinity the last time I dated someone in the industry."

"Oh god. I have three brothers. I threatened to send them a sex tape if they didn't butt out of my sex life."

Lillian blinked. "That was not an approach that had occurred to me."

"It worked pretty well. I recorded a fake sound clip I threaten them with occasionally. It's fun to watch the blood drain from their faces."

"We should definitely hang out more," Lillian said. They exchanged numbers and Lillian walked away.

She felt vindicated. Buzzing with emotion. Cady got it. Sometimes you just needed to able to live your life without other people, even well-meaning people, butting in. She wasn't hurting anyone by keeping this to herself, she was just letting it be. She was protecting her family from feeling like they had to protect her.

# Chapter 29

"I ran into Cady last night," Lillian said. "She says she'll let us know when Zane says he's headed to Bottom's Up."

Xavier wasn't surprised Cady knew. Lillian and Xavier didn't make out in the bar. Well okay, there had been one time she'd come back into the office and things had gotten a little handsy before he'd remembered he was at work. He had certainly discovered plenty of hookups between employees himself. He tended to have a live and let live policy about employee hookups as long as no one was hurting anyone, but he was the boss. It was not the same.

He was happy to be with Lillian and didn't want to poke the bubble, if the bubble was what was letting them continue on, but he had to wonder. "Is there a point at which it gets a little weird that we're keeping this a secret?"

"Secrets are hot," Lillian said leaning over to kiss him.

And okay. He had not found secrets to be hot when it came to his parents. But neither he nor Lillian were married or had kids. They weren't being secretive because anything they were doing was going to be hurtful to anyone. And other than Zane, who'd been working more at Circle now that one of the other bartenders was now recovering from shoulder surgery. So, he and Zane hadn't hung out. Zane had barely had time to stop by Bottom's Up.

And so it had been easy to not be like, oh yeah, I'm seeing someone. But somehow taking another person into the secrecy bubble, seemed bound to make it more likely to pop.

"I do enjoy making you hot," Xavier said. "But hopefully it's more than secrets."

"Oh," she said with a smile that had every nerve ending in his body perking up, "it's definitely not just that." And then her hand reached down to stroke him and well, he forgot to talk for quite some time.

# Chapter 30

"So, Lillian," her boss Georgia said. "Why is HR emailing me about you?"

Lillian froze for a minute. "Oh right, it's because I have exceeded the amount of leave time."

"Okay," Georgia said. "Let's sit down and plan out how you're going to use up all that time this year."

"Well, I had a thought about that," Lillian said.

"I figured you might."

Lillian smiled. "Last quarter is always so huge for us, with giving Tuesday, and all the associated days. So, what if I took every other Friday off in summer. I know we have some end of the fiscal year stuff, so I can work around that, but there's only one holiday for the summer. And that way I'll be there for most of the things, and we might not even need to worry about finding coverage for it."

"I like it. Unofficially, if anyone else asks, I had to think about this for a while because you are a valuable resource, and I wouldn't let just anyone arrange a four-day work week. But I know you'll do you best to make it feel like we're getting you for five days."

"Yes," Lillian said. It was possible she was as much of a workaholic as Xavier. It was wild how when someone complimented you for working hard, she thought, thanks for noticing. Instead of, am I working too hard?

One of the folks she followed on social media had done a few videos about working in non-profits, and Lillian was starting to find it uncomfortably familiar.

But she'd just negotiated a variation on summer Fridays. So now to figure out what to do with all this time.

\*\*\*

From: Friday Ventures
Hey All,
I'm starting this new account because I made the classic error of accruing too much vacation time. In our capitalist society it's often so easy to treat doing things like banking vacation time, as something good. We even call it banking. Sounds like saving would be a good thing, right? Well, not in this case. It's easy not to take time off because there's a pandemic or you can't afford to go anywhere cool. But that's silly. If you're lucky enough to live in the wonderful DC area (and even if you're not) there are so many wonderful things to do. Some of them cheap or free, and some of them costing very little. Sure, it's not quite as cool as jetting off somewhere. But it's more environmental and plus no jet lag.

This summer, I'm going to try and take time to discover and rediscover some of my favorite places to go and be in the area. Calling it Friday Ventures, but of course you can venture on whatever day works best for you. And if you're reading this, I hope you're excited to join me.

So, here's some of the cool things happening around the city this week.

\*\*\*

Lillian had picked a newsletter honestly for plausible deniability. It was much easier to yeet a newsletter off the web and just carry on like it never existed. Also, she thought so much about social media strategy at work, though they had a separate social media person. But all the info she had in her heard about posting times, and audience penetration, made her exhausted. She knew all of that about newsletters too. But she was able to pick a newsletter service that was adorable, but free, but not robust enough for anything they did at work. So, it felt different enough that she just did it.

Lillian: Remember when I said I was thinking about a roundup of stuff to do. Take a look.

Amy: I love it. Oh wow. How do you know about all this stuff? Yes, I know. Research. I like it.

Lillian: Thanks.

Amy: Can I share this with people? Maybe I'll manage to impress my co-workers. Dan's food truck was like the only DC thing I ever knew about before them.

Lillian: Sure.

Lillian felt a little nervous, but whatever. She didn't know Amy's co-workers. And this was the point. In fact, the best way to deal with uncomfortable emotions like nervousness was to power through.

Lillian sent it to a few more people. And Xavier. Who was also a people. But dude you had a situationship with was not just people. Kinda.

Xavier: I like it.

And if now some of her nervousness had gone away, that was coincidence.

# Chapter 31

Torrey was getting wasted at this concert. No, scratch that, Lillian thought, Torrey was wasted. Lillian wasn't one to judge a self-medication choice, and it was a concert. But the White Squirrel was a venue that fit maybe a few hundred people, and they were nowhere near capacity tonight. The band was great. They were a mix of folksy and angsty, with mostly acoustic instruments and drums. Things were intimate enough that the one singer had been chatting with the audience all night.

Torrey had danced to the first few songs, but had gone and done shots until the bartender cut her off, and now had that edge. That edge that said any minute now she was gonna get violent or sad or both.

Lillian had switched to water after the first drink. It was clear one of them needed to be sober tonight, and it appeared it was going to be her. Lillian had been so serious in college. It was partly the whole older daughter, pressure to perform, to prove she could be trusted, that she was on the right path. She and Zane were close enough in age that she could tell her parents were worried about money. So, it felt like anything like getting a bad grade, was not respecting all the time, money, and work they had put into getting her there.

Lillian loved the freedom being at college had offered, but found the looser structure meant she had to sort of build her own, to keep herself on task, on track. She hadn't felt free to do drugs or drink too much, because she was too worried it was going to mess up her structure.

But she had never worried about sex messing her up. In fact, sex had often made her feel more in control, more powerful. Well, sex with the right people that is. Sex with the wrong people did not do that.

"This band fucking rocks! Woo!" Torrey yelled.

Lillian smiled even as she winced internally. It had been a quiet pause between songs so quite a bit of the audience turned to look at Torrey.

"Thanks!" the lead singer said. "Anyway, this next song is our last for the evening."

"Boo!" Torrey said.

"I know," the lead singer said. "But all good things must end. We wrote this song on a road trip when we were all really ready to get back home. So here you go."

A few fans held up camera phones.

"Hey, Torrey," Lillian said. "Did you have a coat or is this all your stuff?" The weather was warming up just enough that Lillian hadn't seen a coat check or anything like that when they came in. Getting Torrey outside and into a cab or rideshare was going to be an endeavor, so she wanted to get a head start.

"Why do good things have to end?" Torrey said.

"Well, some things keep going for a while," Lillian said scanning the area. She didn't see anything that looked like an abandoned coat or scarf or anything. She had worn a knit cowl/shrug thing made of washable yarn, because clubs and handwash was a tragedy waiting to happen. "Do you have your phone?"

"Yeah," Torrey said patting her back pocket.

"Okay, why don't we head over to the door," Lillian said.

"The band's not done."

"I know, but everyone will be rushing towards the door, let's just be closer. How about I call a rideshare for us. Is Arielle home tonight?" Torrey lived in the opposite direction from the club to Lillian's place. But she could either hope the rideshare driver would be nice about two stops, or she could sleep on Torrey's couch or something. Torrey's couch was tiny, but one bad night of sleep wouldn't kill Lillian. It wasn't like she thought going to a concert on a weekday was going to lead to a full eight hours.

"She said if I came here, I couldn't come home," Torrey said. "But I really wanted to come. They're so great right?"

"They are great. Do you want to sleep on my couch tonight? It's very comfy."

Lillian's apartment was an absolute mess. Not the Instagram mess where people were like, oh my god, I'm such a slob. Like, clothes, blankets, paper, tote bags, everywhere. It was scattered in a way that made sense to her, but looked, she understood, absolutely ridiculous. She'd been working on a big project at work, and between that, and all the nights at Xavier's, the Saturday round up of all the scattered things had fallen by the wayside.

But the couch was somewhat clear. Full of discarded cardigans, because her apartment was warm, and so, she'd end up stripping off her sweater on the days she telecommuted and then there was a pile. But that wouldn't take more than a minute or two to clean up. And well, Torrey was drunk, should Lillian's cleanliness or lack thereof really be the focus right now?

"I wanna go home," Torrey said.

"The driver is arriving in two minutes," Lillian said. "We can absolutely take you home if you want."

"I don't get to have what I want," Torrey said.

The car pulled up and Lillian and Torrey climbed in. "Torrey, are you coming to my place?"

Torrey nodded. Lillian confirmed the address for the driver and they were on their way.

# Chapter 32

"Oh fuck," Torrey said. Then a crash.

Lillian peered at her phone on the bedside table next to her. 6:30. Earlier than she liked to be up on a workday, but apparently Torrey was up. Torrey had to be hurting after last night.

Lillian called, "You okay out there?" She slid on a robe. Her sleep shirt covered all the important bits, but it was still a little chilly this morning.

"Yeah, I think I knocked over some stuff."

"Okay, we'll get that cleaned up. Anything breakable?"

"I don't think so."

"Okay, why don't I make coffee. I also have cereal if you want some. I can't remember if I have eggs, but I can look."

"Did we get super trashed and trash your place?" Torrey asked. "I am in so much trouble for not going home last night."

Hmm. Lillian put the first pod into her coffee maker. "Do you have a coffee flavor preference?"

"Got a time turner flavor?" Torrey said.

"I don't think I have that one. Last night you said you couldn't go home. That's why I brought you back with me."

"Did I? Uh yeah, I think, I meant I was going to be in trouble for going out. But yeah, the I spent the night away is not going to go well either. Ugh. I can't believe I made things worse again."

"So, if I'm understanding correctly, Arielle did not want you going out last night. In general? To the concert? With me?"

"All of the above. She thinks you are a bad influence on me."

Lillian smiled. She had liked Arielle well enough the one time she had met her. But well, it was kind of amazing being a bad influence.

Torrey gave her a scolding look.

"Sorry, I've just never been a bad influence before."

"Yeah, well, is that coffee for me? I might as well be awake before I go prostate myself," Torrey said.

Lillian handed over the cup and stuck another pod in to make a cup for herself. "Is there anything I can do to help?"

"No, I gotta do this myself."

Lillian nodded to show she had heard. She had some concerns. They ranged from, I wouldn't have minded pissing off your beloved, but I would have liked to have been informed that's what I was doing to um, why exactly is going to a concert with your friend pissing off your beloved? But she also knew relationships often looked different from the inside than the outside. So, she was going to stay out. Or nearby, but not butt in. After all, she had not exactly given Torrey the full scoop on her and Xavier, so her glass house was, well, it was very glass.

"I can walk you to metro or are you going to rideshare?" Lillian asked.

"Metro, but I can get myself there. I'll try to call Arielle on the way so, you get ready for work or whatever your morning routine is. Thanks for making sure I got somewhere safely."

"Anytime," Lillian said. "Text me after?"

Torrey nodded and grabbed her stuff and raced out.

Xavier: How was the concert?

Lillian: Why are you up so early? I'm mad I'm up this early. Concert was good. Torrey ended up crashing with me, so apparently, I am a bad influence now.

Xavier: For making sure your friend got home safely? I don't think you guys know what a bad influence is.

Lillian: Yeah, probably. I've never been a bad influence before, so I kind of like it.

Xavier: If it makes you happy, then cool. I can think of like much better ways for you to be a bad influence.

Lillian: <Shocked face emoji> Mr. Yang I see we woke up on the innuendo side of the bed.

Xavier: Well, you were out last night so, yeah.

Lillian started to type something about absence and hearts and then deleted it, because that was mushy, and they were not mushy. They were horny. There needed to be a better catchphrase about being horny after being away from someone. How had the catchphrase industry let them down like this?

Something to ponder while she finished her coffee.

Lillian: I need to catch up on work today and actually sleep. But I'll visit tomorrow night.

Xavier: Noted. You could always work from here. I'm working on payroll today.

Lillian: I focus better here. But thanks.

Xavier: Have a good day, bad influence.

Lillian: You too.

Lillian looked around her apartment. She also needed to clean up a bit. Xavier hadn't seemed to mind that they spent all their together time at his place. Lillian tended to meet people elsewhere, even Zane. But now that some had been inside, it became so much clearer how much of a mess it currently was. It just kind of overwhelmed her to figure out how to do more than move the pile of sweaters.

People always said things like pretend someone is coming over, but that never worked for her, because she knew they weren't. She wasn't able to trick herself. She could invite someone over, but why would she when the place looked like this. She'd set a timer after work and tackle a pile or something. If it worked for when she had to focus and write newsletter copy it would work for this too.

Three execs asked her questions about where to take visitors that were come in to do a little light lobbying and fundraising. Lillian had done a bunch of research, and come up with distinct ideas for each of them, so they didn't all end up at the same place.

Her cell phone buzzed.

Xavier: Did you eat?

Lillian looked around the desk area. A plate sat next to her empty tea mug. So, she had definitely eaten something today. But - oh yeah, it was dinner time now. So, she should get more food.

She carried the phone and the plate into her to the kitchen and opened up to see what she had. She grabbed a microwave meal and she stuck that in the microwave.

Lillian: It's cooking now. You work close tonight?

Xavier: Yup.

Lillian: I'll be asleep before you get home most likely. But have a good shift. There's like three sports games tonight, so your sports adjacent customers are gonna be thirsty, I'm sure.

Xavier: Three? Hang on, I'm texting Bailey to check they know where the spare glasses are, and to text me if they need the keg changed.

Lillian: I thought you said if they used the keg truck, they could do it.

Xavier: Yeah, but if they get slammed it takes longer and I can easily run over and do it.

Lillian: You may have a delegation problem.

Xavier: I'm live close. The advantage of being nearby.

Lillian: Bad delegator says what?

Xavier: Isn't that joke older than either of us?

Lillian: I think that just makes it a classic.

Xavier: OK

Lillian smiled at her phone. The food beeped. She carried it to the couch, so she could - well, not exactly not stare at a screen, but at least not stare at the laptop screen for a few minutes more before she finished up.

She pulled up the text thread from Torrey and saw she hadn't sent anything today.

Lillian: Things okay?

But Lillian didn't hear anything back.

# Chapter 33

Zane showed up partway through Xavier's shift. Xavier got his drink and then moved on down the bar to the help the next customer.

Amy and Lillian had been there earlier, but had left before Zane arrived. It was weird. Lillian and Amy could have stayed. Xavier was partial of course, but he thought drinking here just meant you liked no frills bars. It didn't speak to your sex life in any way.

Things slowed down a bit closer to closing, at least enough that he could chat with folks instead of only processing orders, grabbing drinks, and opening and closing tabs.

Zane leaned against the bar. "So, Mr. Watkins mentioned he hadn't found any good renters for the space that used to be Two Bars."

"That's a shame. It's a good spot."

"Have you thought about opening something there?" Zane asked.

"Nah, it's too close to here. I'd be competing with myself."

"Oh come on, that's only true if you do something that draws the same clientele. Come on, we can come up with something."

"You'd want to work with me again after everything?"

"One - obviously. Two - not everything succeeds. Especially concepts that launch right before a world changing event. Three - we ended it well. Not like Vance turning out to owe like six months of back rent on Rock and Squirrel and the employees showing up to an eviction notice."

"Wait what? When did that happen?" Xavier asked.

"Today," Zane said.

Xavier pulled out his phone and texted Claude. He thought about texting Lillian too. But it seemed weird to do that in front of Zane. He'd tell her later.

"Don't think I didn't notice you speak in list form now. Louise is definitely rubbing off on you," Xavier said.

"Sometimes lists are helpful," Zane said.

"How many list apps are on your phone now?"

Zane took a sip of his drink. "Uh, only one. But seriously, if we came up with something that didn't require construction, we could get Two Bars. Well, we'd need a new name, because Two Bars has terrible SEO, cute DC reference or not. And we could try to hire as many of the Rock and Squirrel people as we could."

Xavier paused. It wasn't a terrible idea. Vance may have been an absentee manager, but he did tend to hire great staff. Some of them would already have other options. But if they could present a concept, they might be willing to hang on and wait. Plus Mr. Watkins had said the lease was technically still active, when meant some of the permitting would just need to be amended, not applied for from scratch. They wouldn't be able to open tomorrow, but it could be a faster than normal launch, especially if they went pop-up to start.

"It's too far up for tourists. Circle does the tavern stuff, besides that place's kitchen is tiny, so we'd never be able to do anything like that."

"Well, maybe we go for the other end - people who want a cocktail experience."

"The overhead on the cocktail experience sucks," Xavier said. He liked drinking cocktails, but the combo of the mixology, the fluctuating ingredients, plus the skill needed to make it happen, it was expensive. And then you ended up have to charge a large amount for each cocktail, which both limited your clientele and meant they drank one drink and sat for two hours. But, hmm. "But if we did wine tastings. And you had to reserve a seating."

"Oh yes, take advantage of the seating idea to control flow, and help maximize the limited seating. Plus, we could basically do charcuterie boards as the food, easy to prepare ahead, and then folks get the experience but less mixology experience needed on the part of the staff."

"Yeah, and we could do rotating sommeliers on a consult basis, so we didn't have to stock like every great wine ever."

"Yep, and then the staff can read up on that month's selections. Dude, are you texting Mr. Watkins, or am I?"

"I kind of want to sleep on it. Make sure it isn't late night fumes," Xavier said. It didn't feel like late night fumes. But late-night fumes never did. Not until you woke up the next morning and had to confront what had happened.

"Okay, but text the idea to Claude at least," Zane said.

Claude would love it. Xavier knew that. He wanted to run it by Lillian. "I'll touch base with you tomorrow." And if Lillian liked it, they also probably needed to revisit this secret stuff.

And try not to let her distract him with sex. A difficult task.

# Chapter 34

"Zane came by the bar last night," Xavier said.

Lillian smiled. She knew that, of course. That's why she and her new friend Amy had left. Well, Lillian had left because of that. Amy was dealing with a lot of stuff. Including what seemed like maybe something with Dan.

The DC area was an odd mix. Big important city vibes, and yet somehow some people you just kept getting linked back to, over and over again. "That's good."

"He had an idea. Well, it was kind of a mutual idea."

"Okay," Lillian said encouragingly. Xavier was usually not one to spend quite so much time with lead up. Well, not conversationally at least.

"He suggested we could work together on putting something into the space that was Two Bars. Lanny hasn't found a new renter yet."

"That's cool. You should do that," Lillian said.

"Won't it be weird?"

"Because we're hooking up?" Lillian shrugged. "But he doesn't know about that. So no, it won't be weird."

"It feels like it gets weird to not tell him. All these other people know. Like I know at first it was fine because we were just not telling him. But at some point, not even mentioning it seems like we're ashamed or something."

"I'm not ashamed. I just - my brother doesn't need to be involved in my sex life. Besides. isn't it weirder to start a working relationship with someone by declaring that you're sleeping with their sister? That doesn't seem like the right vibe."

"I guess," Xavier said. "But if he asks about who I'm seeing, I'm telling him."

Lillian had a 99.999 percent degree of certainty that this is not a thing that Zane would casually ask. "Okay," she said.

The expiration date was coming up on this. Amy, who only knew her, and not anyone else involved, thought this was doomed. And Xavier was right. A lot of people already knew.

Probably the only way to keep this up, would be for her to break up with him, because then the desire for someone to spread the news would fizzle. Then she could say, oh we had a thing, but not anymore, that's why I didn't mention it. Then she could go back to her original rules. No bartenders. And if she'd grown a little used to Xavier, to hanging out with him, chatting with him, watching movies with him, well, she'd get over it.

She always did.

But no reason to rush it just because they were thinking about something. It wasn't that she didn't think Zane or Xavier would follow through, but there were a lot of logistics. So, no need to make decisions yet.

That wasn't hiding. Or delaying. It was enjoying the present moment.

# Chapter 35

"Okay," Xavier said. "I actually wonder if I should pay you for this." They had finished the sandwiches Xavier had put together for lunch and now he had gotten his laptop out, but then decided this wasn't an official presentation, so had put the laptop on the coffee table.

"Pay me for what?" Lillian asked from her spot on the couch. Lillian tended to sit like a cat, her legs all tucked up.

It amused him. And distracted him.

"Sorry, that was an incomplete thought. I wondered if we could run the concept for the Not Two Bars place by you, but that's basically like free consulting and maybe I should pay you. Zane and I should pay you. Well, we haven't figured out ownership yet."

"Well, I applaud your instinct, but if you have an idea and you just want me to say, that's sounds cool or that sounds silly, I think I can do that for you on the house. If you want me to like design a logo, then yes, we'd need to talk fees."

"Do you know how to design a logo? Wait, do bars have logos? Do you just mean the sign?" Xavier knew you could do a logo for a bar. He was pretty sure the bar didn't necessarily need one, though this one would be aiming for a trendier crowd, so some basic branding was probably in order. Mostly he enjoyed the indignant look Lillian got when he asked things like is the logo the same as the sign. He would never irritate her on purpose, but occasional indignance, yeah, he was little bit guilty of that.

"I do not only mean the sign, although yes, I think your bar should have a sign. And a better name than Not Two Bars."

"We thought about calling it Capital Concepts because of the alliteration," he said, curious what she would say.

Lillian nodded. "Sure, if you want your bar to sound like an advertising firm."

"Sorry, I just had a flashback to the guy who did a bar that was styled to look like an office."

Lillian cocked her head. "I'm sorry, I thought you said someone made a bar, the thing people go to because they had a long day at the office, look like an office, but that can't be right."

"The menu was designed to look like those old school phone message pads."

"Tell me you are kidding me!'

Xavier chuckled. "I am not. Anyway, yes, we also worried that Capital Concepts sounded like a place you go for a consult and not for fun. We were going to a do state animal, because we liked making it a DC reference. Bar Capitalsauras," Xavier said.

"Is capitalsaurus a dinosaur?"

"Yes."

"There's a dinosaur named capitalsaurus? I never had a dino phase. Is that real or are you teasing me again?"

"I do enjoy teasing you, but nothing I've said is made up."

"I'm not sure which is odder, the office bar or the dinosaur. Like obviously there are dinosaurs in DC. I just assumed they were in the museum where they belong." Lillian grabbed her phone.

"I don't think the capitalsaurus is still alive."

"It's not even a whole dinosaur." She held up her phone. "It's a dinosaur butt. I am going to insist you make the dino butt your logo. This is amazing. An ode to butts. You could have butt contests. Actually wait, what was the vibe you said you wanted the place to have?"

"It was not butt contests. More trendy, hip, whatever the kids call it these days."

"I refute the premise that we are not the titular kids. Titular is quite a word. But back to the point. Or the curve. Get it. Curve of the butt. Anyway, dinosaur butt, if done right, could be an excellent logo. And you could have like an inflatable dino costume person do some of your promo."

"Inflatable dino costume?" It was not butt contests, but Xavier wasn't sure that was the right vibe either. But maybe?

Lillian googled dancing dino, and pulled up one of the videos.

"Oh, I see," Xavier said. "It's just kitschy enough that it might work. Also, a dino butt is basically just a sideways dino, right? Yeah, we could work that into the logo. Are you designing the logo, or you want me to hire the brand person?"

"You should hire a brand person. Let me know if you need some names."

"Will do," Xavier said. Well, he'd gotten agreement from both Yang siblings. Separately. He looked at Lillian and wondered if now was the time to talk about telling Zane about them.

"So," Lillian said. "Are we done with the business portion of this evening?"

Xavier saved his spreadsheet and closed the laptop. "Yes, ma'am."

They could talk later.

# Chapter 36

Lillian: Hey, Torrey, just checking in. You doing okay?

Lillian: Hey, Torrey, let me know you're okay when you get a chance.

Lillian: Hey, Torrey, none of the other knitting folks have heard from you in a bit. And you haven't been showing up to knitting. Just text someone back please.

\*\*\*

"I don't know what to do about Torrey," Lillian said.

"Still no word?" Xavier said.

"Nope." Lillian put her phone on the coffee table. A watched text thread never got replies or something like that.

"You could go over. Or do you know where she works?"

"She telecommutes. As does her partner. So I could go there. I guess the whole problem is that I don't know if she's mad at me - or having to break ties with me or whatever because of my terrible influence. So like, if I go there, do I make things worse?"

"What kind of worse are you worried about?"

"Well, that's the thing, I'm not sure." Lillian had an active imagination, and so she could imagine some very bad scenarios. But she knew the most likely outcome was that Arielle would be mad. And if everything was okay, Lillian didn't want to make her mad if she didn't need to. "I know it's ridiculous, because like I will show up at Zane's with like no warning. Well, I am better about that now. But like if she's fine but not talking to me anymore, then like I hate it but I will deal. Texting someone to tell them you are not talking to them is very seventh grade, but how would I know otherwise? Maybe she lost her phone like Dan and lost all her contact info?"

"Dan got his phone back."

"I know."

"Could you have something sent to her, that has to be signed for?"

"That seems very sneaky and therefore I like it." Lillian pulled up a search page on her phone.

"Thank you. I'll be here all night."

"Yeah, about that," She put the phone down. This could be taken care of later. "Are we gonna talk or watch this movie?" Lillian fake pouted.

Xavier leaned over and kissed her. "I guess we could watch a movie."

Lillian couldn't stop the smile. She sort of liked watching movies with Xavier.

Xavier didn't believe in talking during the movie so she had to save up all her questions and comments until after. It was ridiculous. And yet she had found waiting til the end did make for an interesting discussion. One worth the wait.

# Chapter 37

"We should pick a night to do something," Xavier said. He was packing up the takeout to put it in the fridge. "Or a day. Like a Friday. We could like take the same day off and do something."

Lillian looked up from her phone. "Does do something have like a specific meaning? Or are we talking like bow-chick-a-wow-wow?"

Xavier smiled. "I meant something like we should go somewhere that is not my bar. Together. At the same time." He turned back to the fridge. Exuding casual question as much as he could while he stacked the containers carefully.

"Ah gotcha. We went and grabbed pizza," Lillian said.

"Yes, true. But like we could go see a movie or like a concert or go somewhere the food takes longer than thirty minutes."

"No one wants food that takes longer than thirty minutes," Lillian said. "But yes, I understand what you are talking about. We could do like an outdoor movie. That's always fun. You could really take a Friday off?"

Bailey was back working, and they had managed to hire another employee who had been working out great and had a second job so only wanted part time hours. Things were busy because it was summer and it was light longer. But it also meant he could afford to have three or four employees working some nights. Not all of them, but enough that he didn't have to work every busy night.

He and Zane had been meeting up to prepare for a fundraising push for Bar Capitalsaurus, but they were making good progress. Zane usually worked early on Fridays anyway.

"I could," Xavier said shutting the fridge door. He resisted the urge to wipe down the kitchen counter. They had eaten on the coffee table, so the counter was fine. He tucked his fingers in his pockets. It wasn't much, but he felt like if they could move this relationship outside his bar and his condo, it meant something. He wasn't sure what. But something.

"Oooh, wild and decadent. I'll look around, make a few suggestions and I'll text you."

"Cool," Xavier said. It was a little thing, but he was excited. A day off work and a day with Lillian, it was great. And maybe that would be a better time and place for them to talk about going public. In public.

# Chapter 38

Lillian: Can we get friends and family discount soup and go on a mission?

Amy: I can get soup and am interested in mission. Soup missions. It's legal, yes? Wait, don't answer that on an unencrypted message system.

Lillian: Have you been watching a lot of spy movies?

Amy: Reading spy romances. But also, like reading the news. I know better. So soup. When are we doing the soup thing?

Lillian: Friday good?

Amy: <thumbs up emoji>

\*\*\*

Lillian: Amy and I are going on a secret soup delivery mission Friday.

Xavier: Hope Torrey lets you in.

Lillian: Wow, even Amy wondered what the mission was for like a second.

Xavier: Amy has possibly heard you brainstorming about this slightly less than I have.

Lillian: Possibly.

\*\*\*

# Chapter 39

"You met Torrey a few times, right?" Lillian said, boarding the metro train.

Amy and Lillian found two seats together. Amy's office did summer Fridays. Lillian's did not, but she already had some stuff for this week's Friday Ventures. Plus, it wasn't like she couldn't do things Saturday and Sunday even if a lot of that time had been Xavier time of late.

"Yeah," Amy said. "I met Torrey. She was nice. Is nice."

"She is. Well, so she and I went to a concert and she got a little bit trashed. So, I took her home with me. And then the next morning she was all, ruh-roh, I'm in so much trouble, and also my partner thinks you're a bad influence."

"You?" Amy said.

"Try not to sound so shocked? I have many devious thoughts," Lillian said primly. Perhaps saying such a thing primly undercut the message.

"I'm sure you do. But also like you're a person who encourages people to have fun and to make up with their boyfriends. So like, I would think the partner would be into that."

"Yeah, I only met Arielle once, but I thought we had liked each other. Basically, I don't know if the fact that none of us has heard from Torrey since means she like cut ties with knitting, or like me, and therefore also knitting, or something else. I tried having - well, I did have flowers delivered to them, but Arielle signed for them. So, they haven't moved. But the rest, I dunno. So I decided we deliver soup and they can tell me to my face to go away and not come back, or we can see whatever is going on."

"Got it," Amy said. "I brought extra soup, so we can have some too."

"You're not sick of soup?"

"First of all, how dare you. Second, no. Third, still no. And fourth, not planning to maybe ever be sick of it."

143

Lillian laughed. "The question was not a metaphor for your relationship. But yes, soup is wonderful, and obviously I love soup. But I don't live at the soup factory."

They arrived right as a frazzled dog-walker walking three dogs of various sizes was struggling to get through the door. Lillian held the door open for her and the dog-walker nodded their thanks.

Lillian pulled up Torrey's apartment number on her phone and they hopped in the elevator. The apartment was on the second floor. They made it to the door and Lillian glanced at Amy. Amy gave an encouraging smile.

Lillian: Amy and I brought a surprise delivery.

Lillian knocked on the door.

They could hear scrambling inside and hushed voices, Lillian tried to catch a few words, but it was too muffled. It was the middle of the workday, but if course, they could be in PJs or outfits that were fine if you expected not to be perceived but they might want to change.

They could be in the middle of a work project. A tricky calculation, or on a call with their boss. There were lots of legit reasons you might not make it to the door right away, including hating surprise visits. Which was also legitimate. Lillian hated surprise visits.

So yes, it was hilarious that she was doing this. But also, she was doing this.

It felt like a zillion minutes, but was probably like four, they heard more movement nearer the door.

The door cracked open, and Torrey peeked out, looking, well, like herself, so that was one worry crossed off the list.

"Hey, we're not really set up for guests at the moment."

"Oh, I totally get it," Lillian said. "Amy and I just wanted to drop off some soup. It's delicious. Her person makes it. His name is Dan." Lillian swore she had a better conversation planned in her heard, but apparently it had disappeared.

They handed over the bag with soup. Torrey widened the door a smidge to take hold of it and Lillian caught a glimpse of Arielle frowning. "Oh, also, there's a QR code on there in case you need more soup, or just want to comment or chat with other people who love soup."

"Soup enthusiasts?" Torrey said.

"There are more of them than you know," Amy said.

"Well, thanks, this was super sweet of you guys."

"Oh, it's no problem, though yeah, we would have liked to give you more warning, but the soup..." Lillian had totally forgotten their fabricated soup excuse.

"There was a surplus," Amy said, "so Dan's been having us distribute some to make sure it doesn't go bad."

Right, that was the excuse. It was a good one.

"How nice."

"Torrey," Arielle said.

"So, Arielle has a call about to start, so we have to go. But thanks for the soup. Bye!"

They waved as she shut the door and walked down and outside. On the sidewalk Lillian looked up at the windows, trying to figure out which one was Torrey's. But no, based on the turns they had made, her and Arielle would look out the back.

"So, you got your proof of life," Amy said.

"I did," Lillian nodded.

"And now we are going to go get pastries, or something sweet to go with this soup, because uncertainty sucks."

"It does," Lillian said. "I'm definitely up for pastries."

Lillian just had to hope, that if she needed to, Torrey would use the QR code. And if she didn't, well, uncertainty sucked.

It felt nice to do something concrete though. Lillian's Friday Ventures had found some modest success. Her Fridays off were getting close to the end. And she was going to have to figure out if she wanted to keep doing the newsletter. It looked like she was going to have to figure out what to do with Xavier too.

But for today, she had done what she could about Torrey. The rest she would figure out later.

# Chapter 40

"Hi, Xavier," Mom said. "How much space does your apartment have?"

"For what?" Xavier asked confused.

"What's the square footage?"

"Mom, why are we asking this?" At least she'd called before work this time. Though he had been working on the paperwork.

"Well, your cousin has to move unexpectedly and she needs to store some things."

"They have storage units."

"Oh, those things are so ridiculous. They are dirty, and impersonal, and you have to get your stuff on a schedule, even though it's yours."

"Which cousin is this anyway? Why are they moving?"

"It's Velma. There's something going on with her husband and apparently the internet told her to dump him and move. She needs to store her stuff while she figures out how to afford being single."

Xavier started to ask which part of the internet, but he figured his mom would not necessarily appreciate the subtle difference between say, Tumblr, and Reddit. "Why don't I call Velma and talk to her?"

Xavier suspected his mom might be trying to solve the wrong problem. Velma was in Philadelphia, so he wasn't far, but he wasn't convenient for her. But he could provide moral support, and financial support, if that's what this ask was truly about.

"Oh, you're so sweet. I have her number somewhere," his mom said.

"I have her number."

"Oh good. Now you mentioned something about opening another restaurant?"

"Bar," Xavier said.

"Did you contact the financial advisor I gave you? Did he say it was wise to do that in this environment?"

"I did talk about it with my financial advisor," Xavier said. His advisor was a woman, and had not been recommended by his mom.

He had picked someone his mom would not hound, trying to secretly advise him though the other person. He had also given his mom's name and info to his advisor so she'd know exactly who not to talk to, should the need arise.

"Well, okay. And you aren't dipping into your retirement or anything?" his mom asked.

"No," Xavier said.

"Good. I suppose having two places means you'll be too busy to ever think about kids. You know some of your cousins have four kids right now."

"Four sounds like such a handful," Xavier said.

"It does. I don't know what they were thinking. Four seems cute when they are all babies, but then you have four stinky teenagers, four college educations, it's so much."

"You should make sure they have a good savings plan, Mom," Xavier said. He should feel bad trying to redirect her like this, and yet, he did not.

"Oh, they won't listen to me. None of my sisters will even set up retirement. And of course, you know in another decade they're going to regret it all, and act like I never warned them."

"Mmm," Xavier said. It's possible his aunts had done what Xavier did, gone and gotten their own financial advisors, or googled what they needed and just not told his mom, because they she would advise further. His mom was good at her job, and Xavier was sure her clients appreciated that a lot. But not everyone needed their family to be clients.

It was why a lot of his customers left one place that served alcohol to come drink at his place. It was easier to drink, to relax and be off work, not at work. Xavier figured that was why Lillian came over to his place. She worked from home a lot of days, so her home was her workplace. Xavier's wasn't. That was his theory.

Lillian still wanted to keep things under wraps with Zane. But he had a plan to work on that.

\*\*\*

"You let random strangers into your apartment?" Bailey asked.

"I have a vetting process," Della said. "But also, like weirdos are out there. If my number's up, it won't matter if I went to their place or mine. Plus, what if they have a creepy basement? I know there's not a creepy basement at my place."

"I guess," Bailey said. "I think Tomas and I had been together like six months before I let him see my apartment."

"Different people have different processes. It all works out in the end," Della said. "Or it doesn't. I dated this one woman who like never wanted to go to her place. Well, it turned out her roommate thought they were dating exclusively which we found out when we met for coffee near her place and the roommate happened by."

"Oh ugh. I dated a guy who turned out to not only be married, but like the person who had introduced me to him knew he was married. I had circled back to be like FYI, probably stop setting this guy up with people because he's married. And he was like, yeah, I knew that. And I was like, okay, what made you think I wanted to date someone who couldn't be honest with their spouse about what they wanted. Because if they were polyam, then fine. But they weren't, because polyam people, in my experience are way better about disclosure."

"Not all polyam people. But yeah, like this whole thing where people who don't want to be honest want to claim it's a lifestyle choice, is annoying."

"So true," Bailey said. "Okay, how did we get on this topic?"

Xavier chuckled. "You were talking about your mom rearranging your living room."

"Oh my goodness, I hate it. Like it's been wonderful that she's been staying with us to help with the baby, but I need my couch back where it was. She's all like this will be better for when the baby starts walking. Which is not going to happen for like six months. And also, the baby will learn to walk regardless of where the couch is. Or she won't. But again. Not going to be a couch-based decision."

Xavier asked, "So, is there like some limit of time where it gets to be like a red flag that you haven't seen the other person's place?"

"Xavier," Bailey said her eyes eager, "do you have something to share?"

"I do not have anything to share," Xavier said. The thing with Lillian was still secret, even if his staff all sat somewhere on the spectrum of suspected to knew for sure. But even if they hadn't been officially not talking about it because of Lillian's concerns about Zane, Xavier was not going to talk about his relationship with his employees. But he did have questions.

"I would say," Della said, "like after maybe eight months, I would wonder if there was a dead body. Or an alive one."

"Do you watch a lot of true crime stuff?" Bailey asked.

"Nope, why?" Della asked.

"No reason," Bailey said. "But yes, I would say after eight months it either means there's something at their apartment, they don't want you to see, or..." She gave Xavier an apologetic look.

"Or," Della said, "they don't really think you're a part of their life."

Well, that was a little bit of a gut punch. Xavier was sure there were no dead or alive bodies in Lillian's apartment. And he did understand that sometimes family members inserted themselves a little too far into your life and you had to make evasive maneuvers to protect yourself. The thing with keeping their relationship from Zane was a little annoying. Not because he and Zane talked so much about their personal lives, but more that it took energy to not mention the Lillian parts of his life to Zane.

And there were a lot of Lillian parts to his life these days. So surely that couldn't be one-sided. He couldn't imagine how have all these Lillian parts to his life and she had a life that didn't have Xavier parts.

Technically he and Lillian were not lying to anyone, they were just failing to disclose. But at what point did failure to disclose become something that was another justification for being deceitful? It was hard to say. And if their relationship couldn't survive Zane's interference, if his business partnership with Zane would be affected by this news, then wasn't it better to know that now? Before they started signed paperwork together?

He and Lillian had their big day together planned. They could talk about it all then.

# Chapter 41

Xavier: Surprise! I got here early, so I'm at your building. I can come up if you're not ready yet.

Lillian huffed out a breath at her phone. She supposed this was the universe's way of getting back at her for showing up at Torrey's. Torrey still hadn't used the QR code. Lillian had to hope she was okay. Or not in need of soup enthusiast friends. But yeah, her apartment didn't smell or anything, but it was beyond a little messy. It was be on a reality show about mess messy.

But what was she going to do, make him wait outside when she still had on only a bra and hadn't located her other shoe? Probably not. Her shirt was on the hook in front of her.

Lillian: Sure. My place is a little messy. Try not to faint.

She gave him the number and buzzed him in.

She threw on the shirt. If she could find the other shoe and then make sure she had lipstick, condoms, a mask, and her wallet in her purse she'd be good to go. Her purse was, she scanned the room. The purse was on the counter, so she was okay there. Her shoes were usually by the door, but she had just swapped out some of them and moved them to the closet. She did typically know where everything was. But that seemed to mean that when she couldn't find something, she really couldn't find it. Because the one shoe had been in the closet, but the other was not there, and not in the pile by the door. And she didn't keep shoes anywhere else. Could it be at Xavier's? Surely not.

She had rifled through some of the piles on the living room floor, wondering if the shoe had somehow been taken over by one of them, and had started trying to fold or toss some of the piles into a laundry basket. And then she had lost track of time.

And Xavier was early. Which she honestly should have expected. She had another pair of shoes she could wear. She had lots of shoes she could wear. She had just been set on this pair which was perfect for a day that involved a bakery, a museum, and then dinner. Cute but walkable. Many of her shoes were one of those things. This pair was both. She had this idea in her head of these shoes helping make this day perfect and now she was having trouble letting go of the idea.

Xavier: I'm here.

Lillian tossed the pile into the laundry bag. She'd go back and sort later. There were no shoes in there. Wait, as she got up from the floor, she spotted something under the couch. She kneed over to the couch, grateful for plush carpeting, and reached under. And pulled out the other shoe? How had it gotten there? Well, never mind she had found it.

She opened the door. "Hi, sorry, I just found the shoe I was looking for, and now I'm ready to go. Oh purse. Let me grab that."

Xavier walked in and she grabbed her purse from the counter, checked that all the things were inside. Keys, wallet, condoms, mask, lipstick. Okay. She was set. "Let's go!"

"Lillian," Xavier said in the tone that people used when they were about to deliver bad news.

"I know, it's messy. It's the maid's week off or whatever, let's go." She shut the door.

Xavier followed her down the hallway and into the elevator. On the sidewalk they started in the direction of the bakery.

"Lillian, you're not that messy at my place," Xavier said.

There were a lot of reasons for that. Lillian was better at keeping things contained when there was someone else who cared that things were neat. Lillian had read all the tips and tricks about how to be less messy because she was very good at research. But cleaning was boring, and thankless, and she hated doing things that were boring and thankless. Even to avoid lectures from people who thought they could help. "It's gotten out of control, but I'll get it taken care of, but yes, that is one of the reasons I tend not to invite people over."

"So not a dead body, then," Xavier asked.

"Okay, first of all, rude," Lillian tried not to sigh. "Second, there really must be something more interesting for us to talk about. It's not a problem I need you to solve for me. It's my mess. I will clean it up." And yes, Lillian was aware she'd been saying that for, well, a number of weeks. But also, she knew what needed to be done. She just hadn't gotten around to doing it yet.

"Okay, Xavier said, "did you look at the menu they posted this morning?"

"I did, and I hope we can get a taro donut, because that looked amazing."

"I wonder if it will be taro or ube, we seem to get that all mixed up on the mainland, it's weird.

"It looked purple," Lillian googled taro. "Oh, I see what you mean. Although it might be like mint chocolate chip ice cream."

"How so?" Xavier asked.

"Well, mint chocolate chip ice cream would not be green. Like mint is green, yes, but when you mix mint with milk, it maybe ends up like the very palest of greens. Because milk is kind of like that. But people think mint flavored things should be green, so they put green coloring in it to make it green."

"Oh, hmm. They did a study with Jello. Like if you make lemon Jello clear, people don't believe it's lemon anymore because their brains don't believe that lemon could be not yellow. So it's that whole you eat with our eyes first thing."

"Interesting. But before food coloring, people must have been able to eat things. I wonder how much of it is that whole the red candies taste the best thing."

"You think the red candies taste the best?"

"Obviously," Lillian said. "What other flavors would taste better?"

"Yellow," Xavier said.

"Oh wow, this is something I did not expect from you. I'm not sure we can hang out anymore."

"Okay, but you realize what this means?"

"What," Lillian said already smiling because he had a look that said he had an payoff to this question planned. She loved Xavier's payoffs.

"If we got candy together, you could have all the reds, and I could have all the yellows."

"This is true," Lillian said. "What are your thoughts on the rest of the rainbow?"

"It provides a nice balance so you don't get sick of the yellow before you finish."

"You don't eat in color order saving all the yellows for last?"

"No, do people do that? Sorry, foolish question, obviously some people must." He looked over at her searchingly. "Is that what you do?"

"Oh no, I eat in reverse rainbow order, but I carefully separate all the reds, in case the bag has a smaller proportion of reds and additional maneuvers must be taken."

"Oh, that's wise. You would think with all this technology the candy makers would provide better color balance in their bags."

"I will write to my congress people about this. This is a serious issue, and you are correct."

The bakery sat in a small shopping center, with about ten parking spaces in front of it, and a clear pedestrian pathway over to the storefronts. The storefronts on either side showed signs of construction, and there was a chicken place on the other end.

They ordered enough things that the cashier brought out a box for them. Lillian led them to a small office park fountain area. They sat on the ledge next to the fountain. She flipped open the box, grabbing one of the deep purple taro donuts.

"I'm not sure if it's ube or taro, but it is delicious."

"Yeah, it is delicious." Xavier nodded after his bite.

Lillian ate one of the buns and then a cookie.

"You're not going to eat any more?" she asked.

"I'm good," he said. He wiped his hands on one of the napkins and then carefully folded it and placed it in his pocket.

Lillian shrugged. She ate one more donut, this one was a sesame swirl, the remaining cookies she could eat later.

"Do you just not like sweets that much?" she asked.

"I don't hate them. I just don't eat that many."

Lillian supposed that made it so she didn't have to worry he would eat more than his share. And it was sweet that he'd been okay with her ordering all these sweets when he wasn't that interested in them. But she maybe wished she had known sooner so she could have ordered differently. Lillian thought through the menu. Okay, she actually would not have ordered any differently.

They hopped on metro went down to Union Station. Lillian had read one of those hidden gems that you are sleeping on posts, and while she suspected it was a sponsored post, it mentioned the postal museum. It was one of those places she had seen before, of course. But never been inside. Xavier had said he hadn't been in either. So, they figured they'd check it out. It was a little away - meaning blocks - from many of the other down based museums. But near enough that there were still plenty of things they could do if it turned out it was kind of a bust.

They walked in and wandered through the exhibits. Xavier went through them in order. Lillian found herself sort of flitting across and looking at things that looked interesting and circling back if it seemed related to something else that could provide additional context. It was, as the name suggested, all about mail. Stamps, the history of the mail service, postal inspections, all mail related. Lillian found herself sufficiently done and found a bench to sit on while she waited for Xavier.

Another cookie would be good about now, but she figured the postal museum folks might frown on that. It had definitely been more interesting than she had expected, but she wasn't sure she would call it a hidden gem. She snapped a picture and posted it to her going out account though.

"Sorry," Xavier said, "were you waiting long?"

Lillian shook her head. "It's fine, you were looking at stuff."

"Well, thanks."

She stood and he kissed her. It was a sweet kiss. A kiss that just meant I like you. Somehow a kiss in museum seemed different than the other kisses. Maybe like it was more than a thing. Sure, they had gone beyond the boundaries she usually set for hookups, but it was still just a situationship. A blip, really. Well, okay, it had been longer than a blip. She thought back to the exhibit about the different ways they measured and processed mail.

Perhaps she and Xavier had progressed past situationship into an it's complicated. A non-standard package. Lillian wasn't a fan of it's complicated the way she was of secrets. It's complicated always seemed to end up with someone hurt.

Maybe, this thing between them was unmeasurable, not because there had been nothing like it before, but because, they had passed the point where they should have redefined things.

Lillian was still clear about what she wanted. She wanted to be free to do her thing. She enjoyed regular sex, and didn't mind having sex with the same person. In fact, having sex with someone who knew what she liked was nice. And certainly, having sex with the same person on a regular basis took away some of the necessities of counting, of making sure everyone got off an approximately equal amount of times. Because you figured if it tipped a little to one side this time, it would even out the next time.

But she didn't want a relationship. She didn't want what Louise and Zane had, though they were adorable and she was happy for them. She didn't want what Bailey and Tomas had. She didn't want what Amy and Dan had, or any of the other couples she knew, happy as she was for them that they had found happiness.

She didn't want to present Xavier to her family for their perusal. She didn't want to talk to her mom about her and Xavier's plans for the future. She didn't want to have an awkward conversation with Zane where she tried to find a non-patriarchal way to tell her he would kick Xavier's ass if he hurt her.

And she definitely did not want to have an awkward conversation about why she had dumped him either. It was the double-edged sword of living in a world where everyone expected you to want, to need to couple up. If you did couple up and then walked away from it, well, then now you were really defective. You were the worst. You were that person who went on a dating show and then turned down the proposal. You were ungrateful. You were the reason no one could find a good partner these days. You were all the bad things.

Lillian was a sexually active woman in a society that barely tolerated such behavior. The firewalls were there for good reason. And maybe she had been letting a little too much slip through lately.

# Chapter 42

Xavier was enjoying the day. He so rarely made time to do things that didn't fall into the food, sleep, chores, or paperwork on days he wasn't working. This felt wonderful. It was nice seeing Lillian in new places too. It was always interesting to see what people looked like, behaved like, in different contexts.

If he and Zane made a go of this next project, he'd be right back to most of his waking hours being dedicated to work. There was so much stuff with getting a new place off the ground, even in an initial pop-up stage. The permit list alone was so much. Zane would help of course. And then it would either work or not, and they would make choices from there.

He was never going to stop worrying about it. But he had mostly accepted this new level of worry.

Schism had been about to hit its stride, getting close to being able to have a shift that he or Zane wasn't overseeing when the pandemic hit. The pandemic hadn't been aimed at him. It hit all the restaurants and bars equally. And looking at what was happening with Vance's spaces was proof that the restaurant and bar business remained volatile. Though certainly not fucking your liquor distributor was helpful for maintaining good long-term relationships. Or perhaps not fucking your liquor distributor and other people.

He and Lillian wandered through the Botanical Garden next. He stopped and read all the signs. It was also interesting to know what actually a bougainvillea was versus other things. Lillian flitted ahead and circled back.

After they walked to the Wharf and grabbed lunch at one of the places along the Channel.

"So, would you open something down here maybe?" Lillian asked.

"Maybe," Xavier said. "It's kind of a different vibe. Like with Schism - we were hoping to be close enough to downtown for tourists, but not so far that people who didn't live down town were like, oh that's so far, let's go somewhere else."

"It's funny," Lillian said. "One of my friends at my first job was from Iowa. And she was like, you city people talk about something being an hour away like it's in a different country. It took me longer than that to get to school in the morning."

"It's true. Although, it did also take me close to an hour to get to school in the morning."

"Oh ugh, school bus times were oppressive. I wrote to the County Council about it. They've changed it now. So at least today's high schoolers have it slightly better. But I had to get on the bus at like 5:30. My school wasn't even far away."

"Yeah, the logistics of paying for - reusing the same buses for three sets of schools in a jurisdiction with the eighth worst traffic in the US."

"Yeah. Okay, new less depressing subject. Oh wait, so my original question was I guess aimed at is like your ultimate goal to become a bigger better Vance? Like do you want to own multiple places?"

"I used to think so," Xavier said. "But it's a tough business. And it's hard. Like yes, multiple places can help you serve multiple audiences. But then you also have to track what's going on with multiple audiences. And you have to staff and schedule multiple places to say nothing of city regulations and permits for multiple places."

"Yeah, lots of logistics. And I guess the food hall stuff is more food focused, and less cocktail."

"Yeah, for right now it is. Which makes sense. But hopefully it will turn into something and maybe like with Union Market, and other stuff, it creates places where people can figure out what they want after they arrive."

"Yeah, save the debate and then wander through and pick a place that has space, or has a cool thing. Or you can snack while you wait for another place to have seating and not feel like you're just wasting time.

"Yeah, that's one of the reasons Zane and I talked about doing scheduled seatings. It's not just the cache of being exclusive, it also legit lets people plan, like yep, at 8:30 they will seat us. Instead of showing up and then being told to wait forever. If you have a babysitter, you don't have time to wait like that. And with the apps, like they take a cut of stuff, but they also manage all that so it's much easier."

"That's good. So do you have a next idea for after this?"

"Well, yes, but it also doesn't matter yet. Because if we do this, then we'll have to see how that goes. And how that goes will give me information about any next ideas. So any additional ideas won't make any sense until after that."

"You keep saying if you do this. Is there a chance you won't?"

Xavier wondered if she was hoping that he would or would not. "I guess. I hate to talk about it like a real thing til all the paperwork is signed. But also, I was thinking, we should tell Zane about us."

Her expression didn't change, which was almost weirder. There should be a reaction. She didn't look excited, scared, or nervous, or mad. "Why would we do that?"

"Because, I can't go into business with him again, and not tell him this."

Lillian took in a deep breath. "I don't want to ruin this day. Let's talk more about it later."

Well, that was not terrible. Xavier had expected more pushback. Lillian was smart and thoughtful. Once she had time to realize this wasn't a big deal, she'd realize he was right. He'd love to be able to give Zane a heads up to not be a big lug about things. But whatever Zane's initial reaction, Xavier was sure it would all work out in the end.

They finished their lunch and then walked through the park along the Channel.

Lillian led them to an ice cream place. Xavier got a small cone. Lillian got two scoops. They grabbed iced teas to drink as they wandered back towards downtown.

Lillian reached into her bag. "Ooh, I forgot I still had cookies." She pulled one out and bit into it.

"It's impressive how much sugar you can consume."

"Thank you, I've been training since I was a kid."

Xavier chuckled. He loved discovering new things about Lillian.

# Chapter 43

They hopped on metro and got to the stop where the restaurant Lillian wanted to try was. It was a tiny space, so they only did takeout. But they didn't let you order ahead. Lillian respected the choices, but it meant on days she had to work, it often felt like too many steps to go there and then go wherever she was actually gonna eat the food.

They arrived and there was already a line even though the place didn't open for another thirty minutes.

A few people slipped into line after them. A guy walked up and looked at Lillian. "Is this the line for Oxspoon?"

"Yes," she said.

A few minutes later a woman walked up and asked the same thing.

"Hmm," Xavier said. "I hadn't realized you have an ask me face, but I can see that."

"I have an ask me face?"

"Yep," Xavier said.

"Hi, is this the line for Oxspoon?" another person asked.

"It is," Lillian said.

"We should see how many people ask you before we get inside. I'm guessing six."

"Are you counting the three that already did?"

"No let's start now."

Lillian smiled. "Okay, you're on." She kind of liked this playful side of him.

A rideshare pulled up and dropped off a couple. The guy was wearing a button-down shirt and dark brown chinos. The woman had on a form fitting dress and strappy heels.

"Why is there a line?" the guy asked. He turned and looked at Lillian. "What are you waiting for?"

"I'm waiting for Oxspoon," she said sweetly. Not because this dude deserved sweetness. More because he looked like he had some stored-up ire. And she didn't want it to land on strappy heels.

"Come on," strappy heels said soothingly. "Let's just get in the line."

Softly, Lillian asked, "Does that count as one or two?"

"Oh, interesting question," Xavier said. "I'll say one. She didn't seem like she needed the answer."

"So, I could be at five, but you are being stingy about this. I see how it is." Lillian poked him. He tugged her close and kissed the side of her head.

A few minutes, and one more question about the line directed to Lillian later, a voice called out to them from the front of the line. "Can everybody hear me?"

They nodded.

"Okay, we're going to open and we're going to let in customers in batches of three. So, if you and your friends are here together, you may need to wait because the space just gets too much with more people. You can look at the menu online if you like so that you're ready to go. Also, we love our cash paying customers, but we can do one credit card per order if needed. Okay, we love you all, and we thank you for coming out. First three, follow me."

"What did she say?" Dark chinos called. Lillian could hear people closer repeating everything to him.

"This is ridiculous, you're telling me they are open but we still have to wait to be allowed to go in?"

"The food is really good, sweetie," strappy sandals said.

"There's good food all over this city that we won't have to wait in line for."

"Okay, so you want to leave?"

"Yes."

"Okay, I'll call a car," strappy sandals said.

"Their car is going to arrive as they're practically there," Xavier said softly.

"I know," Lillian said. "It's almost a shame they weren't in front of us."

"Hey," a dude said, "Is this the line for Oxspoon?"

"It is," Lillian said.

The line shifted forward. Seeing people leave with food already made Lillian realize how hungry she was. Lunch had been good, but they'd done a lot of walking today.

The car arrived for chinos and strappy sandals and they left. Xavier and Lillian made it inside and Lillian gave the order they had worked out ahead of time. They ordered four entrees, rice, and two orders of dumplings. There would be leftovers, but Lillian wasn't worried. Leftovers would be great.

Xavier managed to give his card over for the payment first.

"Hey, you paid for lunch too," she said.

"You paid for all the pastries," Xavier said.

"I ate most of the pastries," Lillian said.

"Well, maybe I'm planning to eat all of this."

"Um excuse me, I am definitely eating at least half of this."

"Fine," Xavier leaned in and kissed her.

Lillian was so distracted by that, she missed them calling their names with the food. They grabbed the bags and metroed to Xavier's. They laid out all the food on his coffee table and grabbed chopsticks, and sauces, and napkins, and plates before diving into all this food.

After the first dumpling, Lillian said, "Sorry, brown chino dude, this was totally worth the wait."

"Yeah, it's pretty good," Xavier said.

They got the food put away once they had stuffed themselves.

"So, anything else planned for this epic day?" Xavier said.

"I'm sorry, was all that not enough?" Lillian asked.

"Well, for the most part yes," Xavier said. "I was just checking before I attempted to distract you."

"Oh really," Lillian said. "And how were you planning to distract me?"

"Well, I had a couple of ideas." Xavier leaned in close, pushing Lillian into the corner of the counter, so she could feel him pressed up against her. "But I thought I would start with something like this." He kissed her and this time it wasn't the sweet, light kiss.

This was a deep, yes, I would like to be naked kiss, Lillian felt it warming her from the inside out. She returned the kiss pressing her hip against him, moving her arms around him to pull him tighter, closer.

She tugged his shirt up, and he moved back, helping her remove it, and then remove hers. Her bra went next as they moved in the direction of the bedroom. He shucked his pants, and she stripped out of her and her underpants, in a single swoop. He pressed her against the doorframe, sliding down.

"May I," he asked from between her legs.

She nodded.

He licked into her, swiping his tongue over her clit, and then sucking hard, as he pressed a thumb inside her. She felt the orgasm build inside her and he kept sucking and pressing, and she reached back to grab enough of the doorframe to hold her as she came. He moved to stand, and guided her to the bed. She climbed on. "How do you want to do this?" he asked, sliding on the condom.

"You on top, go fast," she said.

He straddled her and moved inside her. She widened her legs, increasing the angle. They moved together, and she reached between them, stroking her clit and he moved inside her. He pinched her nipple and she moaned again. She came again, fast and hard, and after a few moments, he followed.

They lay there, sweat cooling, and then he carefully removed himself and got up to toss the condom.

Lillian wondered. Earlier today she had been ready to give this up, to end this. But maybe that was hasty. Maybe they could figure something out. Some compromise.

A phone buzzed out in the living area. "I'll go check," Xavier said. "It's probably the bar."

He wandered out naked and Lillian made sure to watch, admiring his butt muscles.

Xavier came back. "Zane's at the bar. He wants to know if I can come talk about stuff. I could tell him I'm busy."

Lillian sat up. "No, you should go. You two can figure out your plans. I'll be fine. It was a great day."

"Are you sure?" Xavier asked.

"I'm sure," Lillian said. And she was. They had a nice day but this was a reminder that things were only going to get more complicated. It was better to end things now, before it got worse. Xavier put his clothes back on and waved as he headed out the door.

Lillian gathered up all her stuff, taking time to look through the bathroom cabinet and the living room. She grabbed all the things she'd left on other visits, gathered them into one of the bags they had used the takeout. She kind of wanted to take some of the takeout with her too, but that seemed mean. She left a note, sticking it on the fridge. She didn't want to text him while he was out with Zane, that would defeat the purpose.

So, old school methods it was.

She thought about saying good bye to the condo, but that was silly. The condo wasn't going to miss her. Xavier would for a little while, but he'd have his friends and his new business and old business. Eventually she would fade into being a person he used to hook up with. And to her, he'd eventually just be the guy her brother worked with. Nothing more.

# Chapter 44

Xavier felt weird leaving Lillian to talk to Zane. She had put him off earlier when he had mentioned wanting to come clean with Zane. But they definitely needed to do it sooner rather than later. It was only going to become more awkward as things progressed.

"Hey," Zane said. "Sorry to make you work on what was apparently your night off, I just, I wanted to get everything nailed down so we could get some of this stuff filed Monday. It probably could have waited."

"It's fine," Xavier said. Sure, he would not have minded staying in bed with Lillian a little longer. But Zane's schedule had been fluctuating a bit. The bartender at Circle was back from shoulder surgery, and back on the schedule. Zane was back to filling in the shifts that others left open. Which meant he didn't always know when he'd have time open. And Xavier had been leaving mornings for Lillian, so he hadn't been as available in off peak times as he normally would have.

They talked through the pieces and got things finalized for the paperwork that needed to be filed.

"So, we're doing this," Zane said.

Xavier hesitated. He wanted to tell Zane about Lillian before they when any further, but her couldn't do that without letting her know. But he didn't want Zane to think any of the hesitation was about him. "Yeah, yeah, we're doing this."

"Cool. I'm excited," Zane said.

"Me too." They of course got drinks to celebrate.

Xavier texted Lillian that it looked like they might be out a little late but didn't get a reply.

He walked Zane home and then got back to his place and standing outside saw all the lights were off. Lillian usually left the living room light on. Inside the apartment, it felt extra empty. He flipped on the light. "Lillian?"

She wasn't in the bedroom. Her clothes were gone. His heart picked up speed, but nothing looked like anyone had broken in, no sign of an emergency. Coming back into the living room he found the note on the fridge. He paused. He needed to know what it said, but the stillness, the quiet of the apartment told him he was going to hate it. He took a breath in and stepped forward to read.

Xavier, I think it's best to end things now before things get too complicated. It's been great. Best of luck with all your endeavors. -L

His equilibrium shifted and he sat on the couch and texted her. They could talk about this. This couldn't be it. This wasn't the time to worry.

Xavier: Lillian, let's talk about this.

He waited, but she didn't reply.

# Chapter 45

Lillian declared Saturday a self-pity day. On self-pity days, one did not have to clean. She did discover she had a cookie left over from the bakery run, and ate it for breakfast. Delicious. She thought about getting more, but that required showers and clean clothes, so in the end she vetoed that. She ordered delivery for lunch.

She waited until Sunday to text Amy. She also texted Helena, Amy's neighbor because Helena seemed like a person who understood wanting to speed through the wallow period and get right into the next phase.

They decided to meet up at the bar near Amy's and Helena's. Lillian probably should have been hanging out at that bar more anyway. It was her need to find an additional bar that had led her to Two Bars, which had led her to Xavier. She should have stuck to the bars that were safe. Or stayed with Xavier a single night and moved on. Maybe two nights. Three max.

Ah well. In the grand scheme of things, she hadn't stolen anyone's money or identity, so they had both come out of the situationship unscathed. Sure, she still felt a little hollow, but that would pass. And now Xavier could go on and be business partners with her brother and not worry about things being sticky or messy. Well, at least not because of her. Bars were often sticky and messy.

Amy gave her a hug when she arrived.

Lillian found herself leaning into it before pulling back. "You're a great hugger, but really, I'm fine." She smiled brightly.

"Or at least you will be," Helena said, "after some alcohol and some quality time with great humans."

"I mean, when has that ever not improved things?" Lillian said.

They got to the bar and made their orders.

"So, what happened?" Amy said. "I thought things were fine."

"They were. But it was going to get sticky because he and my brother want to go into business together and so we ended it to keep that all separate."

"He dumped you because he wants to work with your brother?" Helena asked.

"No, it was mutual. Kind of," Lillian said. She though saying it was mutual sounded better than I dumped him without discussing it. Lillian had made the decision that was best for both of them. It made Xavier's life better, And hers. Sure, it'd be tough for a day or two, but then they could move on. Discussing it would only have prolonged that.

Saying it was mutual even though she hadn't given him a say simplified things. Lillian was a big fan of simplification these days.

"Was your brother a jerk about it?" Amy asked. "Is that why you guys were keeping it secret?"

"He doesn't know. And he never needs to. So therefore, he will not be a jerk about it," Lillian said. "See easy."

"So, it was just like a fuckbuddy thing, secret fuckbuddies?" Helena said.

"Yeah, basically," Lillian said.

"Oh, those can be so fun. It's a shame you had to end it. It can be good to have someone like that you can call when you're in the mood,"

Lillian nodded. She had other fuckbuddies of course. A few had moved away or gotten coupled up, but she still had a few active names. She should call one of them. She ran through the list in her head. Maybe next week.

"I thought you guys had a whole day together planned on Friday," Amy said.

"He did come on my Friday adventure with me," Lillian said. It had been a great day. But it would have been a great day with just about anyone. Okay, maybe not dark chinos. He seemed like a mood killer.

"You spent a whole day not in bed together?" Helena said.

"I mean, there was also sex. But yeah, we went to a museum, and a few other places."

"Yeah, that's not fuckbuddies," Helena said.

"Well, maybe it wasn't fuckbuddies, but it was like a situationship, it wasn't like a whole thing."

"What would have made it a whole thing?" Amy asked.

Lillian sipped her drink. She did not have a good answer to that, other than it hadn't been. There was no way she'd accidentally been in a relationship. She had to agree to be in a relationship for it to be a relationship, didn't she? Surely that was true.

Also, relationships had rules, and progressions, and plans about the future. There were dates and friend introductions, and questions about how many kids you wanted, and if you wanted a house in the suburbs or the city. There were logistics.

So yeah, it hadn't been a relationship. Not really. It had been fun sure. Easy. But that was because it wasn't a relationship. Not really.

"I have questions about the brother," Helena said. "First, if he's single you should always be telling your friends these things. Unless he's a jerk, in which case good looking out. But, not to make this night about me, is the business thing his rule, or yours?"

Lillian sighed. Having a brother, especially a younger brother was so weird. Because society had so primed women to believe the odds were so stacked against them ever finding long term companionship and they had to make use of any and all connections to find the one. Particularly if they suspected the one, they were seeking was male. Starting in high school people had been so excited that she had a brother. And then a little sad when they learned he was younger, though some of them just liked using him for practice flirting, like he wasn't a person. Then post-college, the small age gap began to matter less, and people wanted her to arrange to meet him. As if she wanted to act as a broker for her brother's love life.

And okay, after he had met Louise, she had butted in a little. But he picked Louise without any assistance from her. She just nudged a little when they were having issues.

"My brother is quite happily coupled up, and it's my rule. My brother is a bartender, I made a no bartender rule because the bartender circle in this area is already tight. No offense, Paulina."

"None taken," Paulina their bartender said. "And you're not wrong. It is kind of one big doink chain."

"Really," Helena leaned forward on the bar. "And how does one get entry into this doink chain?"

"Oh, it's not hard," Paulina said. "Probably your best target rich environment would be Bottom's Up, especially Friday or Saturday night. Lots of people end up there, the drinks are reasonably priced, the staff is good, and they are open after a lot of places close."

"Bottom's Up, who was telling me about Bottom's Up?" Helena asked.

Amy gave Lillian a sympathetic look. "It might have been me," Amy said. "Lillian and I went there the night I ran back into Dan."

"Hmm, maybe," Helena said. "Maybe we should go there after."

"Yeah," Lillian said. "Moving on from a bartender to another bartender is not the move I'm going for tonight."

"Sometimes it's the easiest way, get a new sex print stamped in your brain, and your good to go."

"Sex print?" Amy asked.

"Like an imprint, but of sex. Everyone's got moves, go-to's that they rely on. Once you get a new sex print top of mind in your brain, the old one starts to fade."

"Ah, I see," Amy said.

It wasn't a terrible idea. Not going to Bottom's Up. That was a terrible idea. Even if she wanted to see Bailey and Della. But it would be rude to hook up in front of Xavier and his employees. But hooking up with someone new, well, it would help with the moving on. Lillian was running out of bars that were good places for her to go. The other reason she should have stuck to her no bartender rule was that now she had to worry about places where they knew Zane or Xavier. And so, she was going to basically have nowhere safe left. She might have to go back on the apps. Ugh, she hated the apps.

Or she could start looking through her contacts. Somebody in there would be ready to rock. Maybe she'd send out a few feelers tomorrow and see what happened. See drinking with friends was cathartic, and led to great ideas. She'd be back to herself in no time at all.

# Chapter 46

Xavier was having trouble getting himself motivated. After a week of silence from Lillian, and he had accepted she considered the note a sufficient amount of discussion. He knew where she lived and where she worked of course. He could show up and demand she talk to him. But what exactly would that accomplish? If she no longer wanted to be with him, he wasn't going to enjoy hearing her say that live. It wasn't going to help him feel better about it. And he had no reason to believe he could convince her to stay with him if she didn't want to.

He had hoped that day together, plus the hundreds of tiny moments that had come before, would show her they did work, that they had found a rhythm together. One worth continuing. But she had obviously decided she didn't need or want it. And it hurt. But it was her prerogative.

He was showing up to work, and still getting payroll processed, and bills paid, but he wasn't at his best. His apartment was gathering dust, and the laundry was piling up. Both of those things were unacceptable to him, and yet, fixing it seemed too hard. He could hire someone to dust, call a laundry service. But those things cost money, and when you were fundraising to open up a new place, that wasn't the way to show investors you were responsible with money.

He was working late hours, and getting up early to capture all his ideas for the new place. Sometimes that meant he woke up to a text he had sent himself that said, "The glasses should be round". In the cold light of morning this was less of a revelation than it had seemed when he sent the voice note to himself.

He knew he needed to take a rest, take a half day, do something. But he didn't want to have a relaxing day where he strolled museums, or got pastries. All the non-work things he used to do felt like Lillian things, and Lillian things hurt. So, he worked. Because work didn't hurt.

# Chapter 47

Lillian's phone buzzed and there was a knock on her door. She paused folding her laundry and briefly thought, "Xavier?" And then her traitorous heart began pounding.

She had hooked up with someone else and then come home and woken up with the sudden urge to clean her apartment like the adult she purported to be. She had gotten the apartment mostly company ready, thought there were some spots, like under the couch that needed a little extra attention.

Oh, phone. She checked her phone.

Torrey: Hi! It's me, surprise!

Oh Torrey. Her heart sank a little, but that was unfair. Lillian wanted to see Torrey. This was great news. Even if surprise visits, were well, surprising, but not a tradition they should start.

Lillian opened the door. "Hi! I was just cleaning."

"I can see," Torrey said. "And I don't have soup, but okay for me to come in?"

"Yeah. Of course."

They got seated, Torrey on the couch and Lillian on the chair next to it. "Wait, do you need water? Wine? I'm not sure I have anything else. Oh coffee. I have coffee."

"I'm, good, " Torrey said. "So, I need to tell you a bunch of stuff. First, I'm sorry to disappear on you. It wasn't you. Arielle and I were having issues. And she blamed them on you, which wasn't fair, and I went along with it. Not because I believed it, but I couldn't figure out how to fix it, and I couldn't afford to live in that apartment without her, so I figured I go along with it for a while. That wasn't fair to you, and I know if I had told you would have had a better plan than mine, but well, I was trying to solve it myself."

Lillian was still kind of processing all that. "I'm so sorry that you felt like you had no good options. And well, I'm not sure I would have had a better plan, but thanks for thinking I would."

"You made a whole website when you dated a guy who did bad things so that anyone else who dated him would know. You are absolutely the person who would have figured out something that not only solved my problem, but like fixed housing too," Torrey laughed.

"I have not figured out how to fix housing costs. I wish. My best plan there is to date someone who already has bought their place." And she ruthlessly did not think about anyone that might apply to. No sir. This moment was about Torrey. "So, are you and Arielle broken up?" she asked carefully.

"We are. My friend Maya who I met at the cat shelter, helped me sort out a new place to live. It took a while. I'm living in a group house, which is an adjustment, and feels, well it's a little weird. But I can afford it, and it's a better commute on the days I need to be in the office. I lost a lot of my yarn stash, because we decided to move me quickly, but I'll come back to knitting. But you were the one who was kind enough to keep checking on me, which I appreciate."

"I barely did anything. I brought you soup."

"The soup was delicious."

"Well, Dan made the soup. He's Amy, who came to visit with me, he's her person. He runs a food truck. Anyway, I'd love to meet Maya sometime. It sounds like she's great."

"She is. I think you all would get along great. She has like eight jobs, and one of them is working for like an accessory giant."

"Wait, Maya Lian?" Lillian said.

"I actually don't know her last name," Torrey said. But maybe."

"I went to high school with her. We kind of ran in different circles, but she's super cool. Or was. Probably still is, it sounds like."

Torrey tapped on her phone. "Okay, yeah, I just texted her and she remembers you too. She's working at the cat kennel today, but says we can stop in if we want."

"Oh, that would be cool. But so, you're okay now?"

"I'm okay. And I don't mean to make it sound more dramatic than it was. I wasn't like in danger or anything. Arielle didn't even want to steal my identity. She just, it was - we were not in a healthy pattern together. And I could see enough to see that, but I couldn't see how to get out. So, I figured that where I could do what she wanted, even if it sucked, I would do it. To keep things okay, so we could get to a place where I could figure out how to not be there."

"But if she yelled at you for hanging out with me, you not wanting to be yelled at is not weakness, you know that right?"

Torrey smiled, "I'm in therapy. So, I'm figuring all of that out. But yeah. I know that. I'm sorry that I kinda ghosted you. I didn't know how to be a good friend at that time." Torrey looked around. "Your apartment really does look good."

"Thanks. I went out last night and suddenly had the urge to clean everything."

Torrey tipped her head. "I'm not sure if that means the night out was good or bad."

"It was fine." Lillian was in no mood to discuss feelings about one-night stands or how they might lead to a sudden desire to organize one's apartment. "I just had a lot of excess energy this morning and decided to make use of it."

"Okay. That's one of things I'm looking to work on. I've basically been in a relationship since partway through my freshman year of high school, and so I need to get used to being okay with being by myself. Like you."

Lillian smiled. Torrey had missed much of the situationship. But yes. Lillian was free from attachments. She could go out, have sex, and come home, and do whatever she wanted. Which was exactly what she wanted. She didn't need anyone to snuggle on the couch with her, or tell her what movies they should watch. She was fine.

"Should we go see Maya?" she said.

They hopped on metro and went over to the cat boarding place. The place was cute, with whiskers on the sign, and paw print window clings on the large window.

"Hey, Torrey, and hey Lillian! It's good to see you again," May said from behind the counter.

"Hey," Lillian said. "It's good to see you too. I knew you were still in the area, but I think I knew you were working with LuWie and not the other stuff."

"Wait, LuWie?" Torrey said. "Is that the accessory place you work? Their stuff is amazing? Why are you working here? Oh my goodness, sorry, " Torrey mimed zipped her lips, "I promise, I found my brain mouth filter now."

"It's okay," Maya said. "Fortunately, no one else is here today. Well, Nathan, but he's fine. So, yes, one of my jobs is working for LuWie, and I also work here, and, between us three, I also own this place. They call me when a shift falls open, and I get to hang with cats for a few hours, and occasional meet their humans. It's a good gig, if I say so myself."

"Ah, diversifying your interests," Lillian said, basically parroting something she had heard on a podcast.

"Yeah. More like putting money in things I think are cool, but yes, my financial advisor prefers that I call it that. I have a few small interests invested in other things in the area. In the early days of LuWie, we were both working a zillion jobs to cobble together enough money to get things going. I've worked a lot of places, and many of them, I'm happy to never have to work again. But sometimes I gave them a little money to tide things over in exchange for a small partnership stake. Or In the case of this place, I bought it outright from the owner when she wanted to retire."

"Nice," Lillian said.

"Wait, you let me work here," Torrey said. "I didn't know you were the owner."

"Surprise," Maya said. "I don't tell most people because they get weird about it. Fiona's still the manager."

Torrey nodded.

"Wait, Lillian," Maya said, "aren't you Friday ventures?"

"I am," Lillian said.

"Okay, then you are the perfect person to ask. There's this place that's looking for investors. They want to do like limited seatings, wine flights, with rotating guest sommeliers. That seems like a hole in the currently market, yes?"

Lillian kept her smile bright even if she felt like someone had poured a bucket of ice over her, leaving her breathless and cold. "Capitalsaurus Bar. And that's my brother and his friend, so I am biased, but I think it sounds great." It felt like every day the ways she would be reminded of Xavier were new and exciting. Eventually she'd get used to hearing about the place.

"Oh, Zane. He was a few grades below us. I should have looked closer at that. I looked up Xavier, but he went to a different school."

Torrey gave Lillian a look Lillian wasn't able to decipher, and was sure she didn't want to decipher.

"Well," Maya said, "I have like an hour more before Fiona gets here. If y'all want to grab dinner or something after I'm game. You are welcome to hang out here, but the only good seating is in the cat room."

"Actually," Torrey said. "I feel like we might need some cat therapy."

"What's cat therapy?" Lillian asked. "Does the cat ask us about our childhood?"

"Let me check with Nathan," Maya said. "You know how to behave yourself around cats, right?" Maya looked at Lillian.

"Yes," Lillian said, though she suddenly felt like she had forgotten everything she had ever learned about cats. Cats, they had fur, right? She was sure of that part. Wait, most of them had fur. There were furless ones too. Did the furless ones like being pet? She guessed she'd find out if they had one.

"Nathan? Who've we got up next for playtime?"

"Xena, T'challa, Hulk, Regina, and Precious."

"Oh, that's a good bunch, and they like new people. Well, except Precious. But she won't hate you, she'll just probably ignore you."

Maya led them back through multiple doors, into a large room with a few benches, chairs, a couch, and several cat trees. "Don't sit in the chair," she pointed to the one cushioned chair, "Precious loves that one, but anywhere else should be good."

Lillian really wanted to sit in the chair. But that was being contrary. So, she sat on the couch like a mature adult. She wondered if that had been the problem. She had made a rule, no bartenders. And then part of her had been waiting for a good reason to break it.

Sure, the first time she and Xavier had hooked up, she hadn't even known she was breaking the rule. But she had known after. She had known after Thanksgiving. And so, here she was, and any pain she felt, it was her own fault. Because she had made a rule based on the smartest safest choice. And then she had gone and broken it.

The cats were allowed into the room and sure enough Precious, or so Lillian assumed the tabby cat who went straight for the chair and curled up was, settled in. And Precious looked so content in the chair, Lillian felt bad for even having briefly thought about sitting in it. See, her chaos monkey instincts were bad. She should definitely corral those.

Two of the cats were each climbing the same cat tree. Torrey had started tapping her hands against the seat of the bench she was on and had attracted the attention of one cat.

"So, that guy, the one who's going into business with your brother, that was the one you hooked up with, right?" Torrey said.

"Good memory," Lillian said. So much for thinking Torrey had been to focused on her own drama to remember Lillian's.

"So, is it awkward that they are going into business now?" Torrey said.

"No," Lillian said. "We had a thing, but it's over. And this bar will be good for both of them. I hope everything works out just like they wanted." Lillian smiled. Because things you said when you smiled, it was like asking the universe to make it so. If the universe could hurry on getting her used to smiling and talking about Xavier, that would be great too.

# Chapter 48

Xavier's head pounded and his stomach swirled with nausea. Alcohol, his livelihood and also, sometimes, a curse. They had gotten the last permit approval for Bar Capitalsaurus, and the first week of seating was booked for next week. They had thought about doing a soft open, but had been advised that calling the first week premier week, was more likely to sell them out. And it had.

He and Zane had both been off schedule at their respective places, and so had gotten very, very trashed in celebration.

Xavier cracked open an eye gingerly and looked around. No strange people. He was in his apartment. And no signs of bodily fluids in places they shouldn't be in the bedroom. Well, that was a relief. He slowly got up and wandered in the kitchen for water, since drowning any lingering alcohol in his system was the way to go here before adding any food. Everything looked normal in the living/kitchen area. He definitely remembered spending part of the wee hours hunch over the toilet, but maybe he was past that part of things.

He chugged a glass of water, poured another, and chugged that too. He poured a third, but he'd go a little slower with that one, so carried it over to the coffee table and rested on the couch.

He checked his phone.

Louise: Hydrate well, Dude. If you got even half as toasted as Zane, you're probably still half drunk.

Xavier: [glass emoji] Team hydration.

He usually tried to not get that trashed not just because the recovery period sucked, but also because he didn't want to get used to feeling numb.

Numb was really attractive right now, and he knew that was bad. It was probably something he should consider therapy for. He'd tried time and alcohol both, and they hadn't made the part of him that missed

Lillian miss her much less at all. It hadn't made him stop wanting to share every success with her.

He didn't think it had anything to do with working with Zane. When Xavier looked at Zane, he didn't see any of the things he loved about Lillian. Zane didn't have her infectious energy, her ability to change the subject on a dime, her hair, or even her smile. There was one expression Zane made that reminded him of Lillian, the, I think you are being an idiot but I am going to humor you expression. But otherwise, it was like they'd each gotten a different half of their parent's genetics.

So, it wasn't Zane that was reminding him of Lillian. Or not more than everything else. was.

The staff had been kind enough not to mention it, but they had all certainly noticed that Lillian hadn't been by.

He looked at his phone again. The text thread with Lillian was lit up. When he flipped over, there were no new messages from her. Wait, no. The screen stuttered and then refreshed. Oh no.

Apparently last night he had sent her like twenty new messages.

Xavier: Lillian, you're the best.

Xavier: Lillian, I miss you.

Xavier: Lillian, we could stay secret forever if that's what you really want.

Xavier: Lillian, we should talk.

Xavier: Lillian, I miss your laugh.

Xavier: Lillian Lillian Lillian

Xavier: Lillian is such a pretty name.

Xavier: You know our names both have three syllables.

Xavier: Yours has more letters though.

Xavier: Having more letters doesn't make you better.

Xavier: I take it back, you are better. You're the best.

Xavier: Best. Better than all the rest.

Xavier: Hey, Lillia, You up?

Oh wow. Someone should have taken his phone away. Well, if Lillian hadn't blocked him by now, she probably had after this. Part of him wanted to text, "I was very drunk and I'm sorry", but that honestly felt like trying to put out a fire with gasoline. He should delete this text thread.

Lillian had executed a multi-step plan when she wanted to get in touch with Torrey. Lillian knew where to find him if and when she ever decided she needed to talk to him. He needed to leave her alone.

He changed her contact in his phone, to "Leave her alone". And he finished his glass of water.

# Chapter 49

Zane had bugged Lillian to come over and raid their fridge. It was hardly raiding when you had an invite, but Zane did make food she liked eating.

On the sidewalk in front of Zane's place, Lillian took in a deep breath before texting. She was excited to see Louise and Zane. And Zane was of course going to want to talk about everything going on with Bar Capitalsaurus because he was excited about this new venture as he should be. It was a huge deal, and she was super excited for him. Their mom had already told all her friends that their first week had sold out in an hour.

Lillian: I'm here.

Zane opened the door and she toed off her shoes, before remembering that Zane didn't really do that. Oh well, it would be weirder to put them back on now.

"Where's Louise?" she asked.

"Louise is meeting with one of her friends tonight. So you just get me. But I made soup," Zane said.

"Oh well, I guess I could stay for soup," she said with a smile. She liked Zane. But had kind of been hoping for Louise to give her someone to talk to who did not want to talk about bartenders. Well, it didn't matter. She was fine. She'd be fine with Zane. "What kind of soup?"

"Carrot and bean," Zane said.

Lillian nodded as he ladled out the soup and also put out a small salad. "Wow, salad too? We are fancy."

"We've been working so hard on everything for dinosaur butt. Crap, I have to stop doing that. I'm going to slip up in front of a customer."

"Dinosaur butt?" Lillian asked, as if she didn't already know.

"Yeah, the capitalsaurus isn't like a whole dinosaur, they only ever found the butt. So, we started calling it dinosaur butt, as a joke, but well, clearly I need to stop doing that."

"I don't know, dinosaur butt has a certain ring to it." Lillian took a spoonful of the soup. "This is delicious, Zane. You sure you shouldn't be starting a soup business?"

"No, Dan, one of Xavier's employees started one, so that's taken care of. Besides I like soup being my off-time thing. Kind of like your newsletter."

"You read my newsletter?"

"Of course I read it. It's really good."

"Thanks," Lillian said. Lillian had of course sent it Zane and their mom. But she somehow had figured they would say it's nice and then never read it. Or something. She wasn't foolish enough to say something on the internet that she didn't expect her family to ever find out about. But she also figured her mom had probably read one, and then told her friends that Lillian had a podcast or something.

Zane caught her up on various stories involved with getting the final steps of Bar Capitalsaurus up and running. As they put the rest of the soup away, and he packed a to go container he insisted she take home, he asked, "So anything else new with you these days?"

"Nope," Lillian said. "Just same old, same old."

"Okay," Zane said. "I'm going to say one thing, and then I'll butt back out. But my business partner has been moping like his heart's been broken. So, if there's anything I can do to help out with that, let me know. And if it's none of my business, that's fine too."

Lillian froze. She understood the words of course, but they only made sense if - but maybe this was a test. Or maybe, like everyone had been telling her all along, she wasn't as good at secrets as she liked to think she was. "You knew?" she asked.

"Yeah, but I know I went a little overboard after dickhead two, so I stayed out of it."

"How long have you known?" Lillian asked.

"Since New Years. Louise suspected at Thanksgiving, but I told her it couldn't be. Had to apologize for that."

So, yeah, Lillian was much less slick than she had though she might be. Of course, Cady apparently had thought that Zane didn't know. Or maybe Cady had been stringing her along. Lillian hadn't ended things entirely because of Zane, but wow, it turned out she'd had protected very little of anything by keeping this under wraps.

"I wasn't trying to hide it so much as keep a good boundary between my sex life and everything else."

Zane laughed. "Well, I appreciate that on the one hand, because while I wish happy things for you, I don't like to think too deeply about your sex life. But I'm sad I ruined things with dickhead two. Well, okay, I'm not actually sad about dickhead two. But I am sad that you felt you couldn't trust me with this." He slung an arm around her shoulder. "I just want you to be happy."

"I know that. I want the same for you. Mostly."

"Mostly?" Zane asked, voice filled with faux outrage.

"Well, I also want you to stay humble."

"Oh, okay," Zane nodded. "Good looking out."

She left Zane's place with her to go container of soup and paused on the sidewalk. Going right would take her back to metro. Going left would take her to Xavier's. But what would she tell him? It turns out Zane knew all along, but also, I still don't want marriage and babies and all that? Zane knowing didn't change much. Not really.

Because Lillian still didn't want to be locked into something that required a level of strategery to get out of. It was easier to be footloose, the rolling stone, all those metaphors for things that did better on their own and not coupled up. And if she still missed him, she would just fill those holes with more fun, more excitement. She should work on having so much fun she didn't have time to miss him. After all, she was the fun expert.

# Chapter 50

"Hey, Lillian," her boss Georgia said. "What's a good place to take this donor from Texas too?"

"Well, there's this new modern Indian place."

"Can't be Indian. He ate Indian once and got food poisoning and will now eat anything but that."

"Asian fusion? It's in Logan Circle."

"Oh, that sounds perfect. Email me."

"Will do."

Lillian couldn't imagine cutting out an entire cuisine because of one bad experience. Never eat at that restaurant again, sure.

Oh crud. Lillian felt the uncomfortable chill of self-realization.

Her first serious relationship, she had given her all, trying to be the most perfect future wife. And he had tried to steal her identity. He hadn't wanted a future with her. In the aftermath, after she'd set up the website, and had quite a few self-pity days, she'd done some self-reflection. And realized, the picket fence stuff she had thought she wanted with the ex, was actually not what she wanted. She wasn't sad that she wasn't married to him. She wasn't sad that she wasn't married to anyone.

And so, she'd focused on hookups. But people kept telling her she must want more. Whether it was Zane going over protective brother, her mom, the knitting crew, everyone kept telling her she must want something more than what she had.

And so, she had been calling what she had with Xavier a situationship so no one would think she was asking for more.

But the only thing Xavier had ever suggested changing was who knew. He hadn't tried to change her, or push her towards marriage or kids. He just wanted to be able to tell to people about them

Lillian scanned her contacts list, and found herself scrolling down to Xavier. Maybe, if everyone, except maybe her mother, had known about her relationship with Xavier, its success hadn't been predicated on supposed secrecy.

And maybe she had kept calling it a situationship, but as Helena had suggested, it wasn't. It wasn't an it's complicated. It had been a relationship. So maybe the relationship she wanted existed, as long as she let it. Maybe it wasn't only able to be a success in secret. And maybe, Zane had been a teeny bit right, that by keeping it from him, she didn't give him the chance to be a good evolved brother about it.

Because, Lillian missed Xavier. She missed hanging out with him, at the bar and at his place. She missed watching movies with him, and eating food with him. Maybe he felt the same way.

Of course, despite Zane's assertion that Xavier was wrecked, Xavier worked in a target rich environment. Xavier could forget his feelings any day any time he wanted. He was probably just about ready to move on.

But, no defeatist thinking. She could make an offer. And he could decide what to do. She would just have to figure out what to do. But maybe this time, she would actually enlist a little help.

Lillian: So, awkward question.

Amy: My favorite kind.

Lillian: If I wanted to try and make up with someone, how does one do that?

Helena: You can always strip naked and hop on their bits. 97 percent success rate.

Lillian: I'm gonna need to know, is this rate based on personal experience, or did you do a survey, read a paper?

Helena: Okay, math nerd, I didn't really do the calculation. But I've done it eight times. And it worked seven. The eighth time like half worked.

Amy: How would it half work?

Helena: We got off, but she kicked me out right after. So I got what I wanted. But no repeats after that which was a bummer.

Lillian: Fascinating. And Amy, did your approach also involve nakedness.

Amy: I brought soup. But eventually there was nakedness.

Lillian: You brought Dan, soup? Okay, I think I can work with that. Thanks all.

# Chapter 51

"So, thanks," Velma said. "I appreciate all of this." She gestured at her suitcases in the living room. The rest of her stuff had gone into storage.

"It's no big," Xavier said. "You're family."

"Okay, let's not do that," Velma said. "We all know that I talked to my mom, cousin Nene, and they all said that sounded hard but didn't do anything."

"Well, if it helps, I'm guessing your mom called my mom, who called me. So partial credit?"

"I guess. I know you know from messy family ish. I'm sorry - belatedly I realize, I wasn't much help when your parents split."

"You were in high school."

"Yeah, so I was a self-absorbed teen. But I had internet. I could have called you more."

"You were fine. There's only so much you can beat yourself up for stuff you didn't do."

"Well, this," Velma pointed to the stack of boxes in the living room, "is what's left of stuff I did do. So not feeling great about that either."

"Okay, this is a bad line of thought. Wanna come see the new place. We have to meet a city inspector tomorrow, so I want to double check that everything is where it needs to be."

"Sure," Velma said.

They walked over to Bar Capitalsaurus, or dinosaur butt as Zane kept calling it. He showed Velma the sleek space they'd managed to cram 25 seats into by tearing out the bar, and leaving only the backroom and a small host nook. Xavier's phone buzzed. "It's Della. I need to go over to the other place. You can come with, or do you have your keys?" He tried not to think about the fact that Lillian had never wanted keys.

"I can come with."

They walked down to Bottom's Up. Xavier introduced Velma to Della and Bailey who smiled. "The cider guy says you have to sign off on the order," Della said.

"Is he still here?" Xavier asked.

Della nodded.

Xavier checked and signed off the order. He came back in. "Sorry, about that. Apparently, he had a bad experience and was being paranoid. I told him you are able to sign off on the orders too."

Della nodded.

"It's a good thing you'll be close, because I think we're going to have to do that with each of them."

"Nah," Bailey said. "I mean it is nice that Xavier has such a sweet commute. But there's just the liquor distributor, and he's not nearly so uptight, and then the cleaning and bathroom supplies distributor, and they let anyone sign off. I've signed off tons of times." She looked over at Xavier. "After I checked the order of course."

"I know," Xavier said.

"Do you do food here?" Velma asked.

"No," Bailey said. "We're bare bones here."

"Bummer. Because I totally want to pick your brains, but I am so hungry."

"I can order some takeout to go back to my place," Xavier said. "Our place."

"Nah, it's still your place. You're just letting me crash. Okay, it was nice to meet you all. And now that I know the way, I'll be back."

"It was nice to meet you."

They all waved.

"Text me if anything else happens."

"We will," Della said.

"But it won't," Bailey said.

"Oh my goodness, knock on wood before you say stuff like that, girl," Della said.

Xavier chuckled and waved.

"So," Velma said, once they had put their food order in. "Big believer in a short commute?"

"Well, kinda. I found Bottom's Up first, and then when I saw this condo was for sale, I kind of went for it, figuring if I was close, I could be there easily when stuff happened and I could go home easily after a late night. Lanny Watkins, who owns the lease on Bar Capitalsaurus, he lives nearby too. When his last renter bailed partway through, he offered to give me a good deal to put something in there."

"So, you do just kind of collect people," Velma said.

"Well, I own a bar. I allow people to pay me for alcohol."

"But it's not just alcohol. It's community. Like I bet you know which of your employees are dating and all that."

"I mean, I do. But that's because they tell me that stuff."

"Okay, but my manager couldn't remember that I was married. Even though I've brought my husband to multiple company events."

"Well, your manager sounds like kind of a jerk. And your husband."

"Yeah, yeah, he's a little forgettable. But you've built a community. And now you're making it bigger. That's kind of great. So why are you so sad?"

Xavier shook his head and laughed like that was the funniest thing he'd ever heard. "I'm not sad. Busy, but not sad."

"Okay, we don't have to talk about it. I'll go over and ask Bailey. I bet she'll tell me."

She would. Bailey and Della and Dan and Mateo had all been super solicitous. Even if Lillian's absence from the bar hadn't been a sign, he was sure Lillian had told Amy and Amy had told Dan. Who had likely mentioned it to Matteo, and so on.

"It's not a big deal. I was dating someone. It didn't work out. And here we are."

"She broke it off, or did you?"

"She did," Xavier said.

"I'm sorry. And here I am with the remnants of all my stuff."

"You are not making me sad. I'm not even that sad. I'm...," he struggled to find the right words, "processing. I have a good life. I'm fine."

"You do have a good life. I'm sorry she didn't want to be a part of it. Maybe she's got some growing up to do."

Xavier nodded, though that didn't seem right. Lillian was plenty mature. Maybe he thought her having strict family/not family boundaries was limiting, since eventually your people became your family. Or something like it. But he didn't want to talk about Lillian. Talking didn't help.

He wanted to eat food, and get permits approved, and solve the problems he was able to solve. Lillian wasn't solvable. Not for him.

# Chapter 52

A package sat on Xavier's doorstep. He picked it up and carried it inside placing it on the kitchen counter. He was ready to fall asleep, having worked at both Bar Capitalsaurus, and then having checked in at Bottom's Up after. The staff at both were handling things well, but there were always tons of tiny little things, getting all the cases unpacked, broken down. Making sure all the scheduled deliveries had shown up, all the kegs had been checked. And at Capitalsaurus, there were often times when being able to step in and say, "Hi, I'm one of the owners, is everything okay?", smoothed things over. Or not. Some people really thought they could arrive to the second seating barely able to stand and still get served.

He'd go change his clothes and then take a look at the package.

In the morning, he stumbled out to grab some coffee and saw the package. Oh right.

He decided to make coffee first. But while the coffee brewed, he looked. There was no return address. Okay, that was weird. It was wrapped in brown paper, which he didn't think anyone who wasn't his grandmother still did.

He grabbed some scissor and sliced the paper off. The box inside had a bunch of crossed over addresses, including one in Silver Spring. Some eighty thousand people lived in Silver Spring, but his first thought was Lillian. He sliced through the tape and inside were two bottles of wine and a card. Huh. He opened up the card carefully.

Xavier,

I'm sorry for ending things without talking to you. I'm sorry for ending things at all. I let my worries about what other people would try to make us get in the way. I know buying alcohol for someone who has access to liquor distributors is a lot. But well, it turns out there is taro wine, though it's Palauan. The second bottle is Hawaiian. I hope you find time to enjoy them.

I ~~miss~~ wish you well.

Lillian

Xavier kept staring at that crossed out word. Did it say miss or did he have overly hopeful eyes?

Okay who was he kidding, he was definitely texting her no matter what the word had been.

Xavier: Got your gift. Thanks. And if you want to try either or both of these bottles with me, let me know.

When bubbles didn't immediately show up with a response, he put the phone on the coffee table and went back to finish pouring his coffee.

It was buzzing when he returned.

Lillian: Your place, an hour good?

Xavier: Sure!

Xavier scanned his apartment. Velma was back in Philly for a few days wrapping things up. And he had kind of let things slide again. He immediately started racing around picking up clothes, papers, blankets. He was about to stuff everything on the bed to be sorted later, and then cringed. What if, well, maybe the bed should look good too. He tossed all the clothes in the closet. The papers he took back out to the desk and, with a small sigh, because they had been somewhat organized, he stacked them all together in one big pile. It wouldn't take long to re-sort them on Monday. Probably. He was still chasing around when his phone buzzed again.

Lillian: I'm here.

He looked down. He was still wearing sweatpants and nothing else. But he wasn't going to let her wait and think he had changed his mind. Obviously, they had some stuff to talk through, but if there was a chance to take her back, he was taking her back.

He opened the door. "Sorry, I'll go grab a shirt. I was cleaning and got distracted. Hi."

"Hi," Lillian said. "Go grab a shirt, I can wait."

He opened the closet and tried to find a shirt that looked okay, and threw it on before coming back out.

"So, the wine is there. Did you want to try it now?"

"Xavier," Lillian said. "Sit, the wine is an excuse."

Xavier sat.

"So, I know leaving with just a note was kind of a jerk move. And I wanted to say I'm sorry. For leaving like that. And for leaving."

"I read the note."

"Okay, well, I wanted you to know. And I was worried."

"About Zane, I know. You don't have to tell him. Like it might eventually get awkward, but we can go at your pace."

"Well, Zane knows actually. But that's kind of my point. I was worried Zane knowing would change us. I didn't want to have a relationship that was restricting or people always talked about like how falling in love is such a great thing because you become vulnerable. And honestly, after the ex who tried to steal my identity, I felt like that was stupid. I didn't want vulnerable, I wanted to be in control."

"I get that."

"But if I had paid attention to us, I would have seen that being with you wasn't making me less, and I didn't need to give you up to stay myself. So that was my baggage, and I'm sorry I did that to you."

"Okay," Xavier said.

"So, did you want to try again maybe?"

"More than anything?"

"That easy?" Lillian said.

She stood and he stood and suddenly they were pressed close together.

"I tried being without you. Not a fan."

Lillian smiled. "Same here. Can I kiss you?"

"Please do," he said. Their lips met and it was like coming home, like tasting your favorite dessert that you hadn't had in a while, it was both just as he remembered, and better because it was here, now.

It was a good thing he'd cleaned off the bed too.

The end

# Acknowledgements

Thank you, as always for reading.

While I do often connect my stories because there are only so many fictional DC's that can live in my head, I really had no intention of writing this story. Sure, I had given Zane a sister in *Hot Bartender*. And well, I had given Zane a bartender friend named Xavier. And then in *Troubled By Love,* I needed Amy to have a hobby. So, I picked knitting, and Lillian had been knitting, so why not have Lillian be the friend she meets through knitting.

It often sounds very weird to say that my characters told me a thing, or that I discovered a thing about them when typing. Obviously, I am the typist, so it was my brain that invented the thing. But when I am deep in storytelling mode, it can sometimes feel like I plucked a plotline out of the ether and it just happened. So, I was delighted to discover that Lillian was hooking up with Xavier. And then, realized that I was going to have to write that story.

It does turn out that when you write a story that overlaps a timeline of another, the timeline is a huge mess. Yes, this story does start before *Troubled By Love,* and end after it, and yes, I did that too myself.

And then did I stick Maya in there, who appears briefly in *Bored by the Billionaire,* because I cannot stop myself? Yes, yes I did.

Thanks again for reading. I started thanking all my English teachers in my first book, and it seems foolish to stop that now. So, thank you to all of them.

Thanks to the local DC writers who planned virtual meetups that allowed me to get on and write the second I logged out of work. Thanks to the New York kid lit writers, and New Zealand writers who did the same. Thanks to the Global Write In Crawl, which planed a weekend where I got to write with folks around the world, even if the Maryland writers wrote later than my sleepy self could stay up for.

I am the most enormous crank when I am editing, so thank you to everyone who puts up with me during that part of the process.

Reviews are always helpful, so thank you to every reader who tells someone about a book they loved or even didn't. Please consider leaving one on your site of choice.

I love hearing from readers. There's a contact form on my website, a newsletter, and I can often be found on BlueSky these days. Feel free to reach out to me.

Newsletter for info on new releases and what I'm reading and writing can be found here: https://buttondown.email/talkapedia

ARC team signup is here: https://forms.gle/rXz2iqt6VaR8aq6F7 [1]

---

1. https://forms.gle/rXz2iqt6VaR8aq6F7%20%20

# Also by Tara Kennedy

City Complications Series – Adult Contemporary Romance:
   *Aloha to You* –Novella
   *Undercover Bridesmaid* –Novel
   *Hot Bartender* –Novel
   City Entanglements Series: Adult Contemporary Romance:
   *Repeated Burn* – Novella
   *Bored by the Billionaire* – Novella
   *Clear as Ice* – Novella
   *Not an Ending* – a bonus epilogue available to newsletter subscribers
   *Of Kings and Queens* - Novella
   Too Busy Romance series: Adult Contemporary Romance
   *Troubled by Love* – Novella
   *Tricked by Love* – Novel
   Standalone Short Stories
   *Bait Girl* – A Young Adult Short Story
   *Called to the Water* – An Adult Fantasy Short Story
   *Dreamcatchers Anthology* – A multi-genre, multi-author collection
   Non-Fiction:
   *Let's Talk About Fictional Sex*
   Find info on where to buy them at: www.tarakennedy.com/books[1]

---

1. http://www.tarakennedy.com/books

# About the Author

Tara Kennedy is a lifelong Washingtonian of Hawaiian, Chinese, and European descent. She wrangles data by day and writes in her spare time. She has dabbled in audio narration. Tara had a short story published in *Commuter Lit*, and in an upcoming anthology. In addition to short stories, Tara also loves writing romance. Information on books, blog, and newsletter can be found at www.tarakennedy.com[1] and Tara can also be found on BlueSky as TaraTLK.bsky.social

---

1. http://www.tarakennedy.com

# Troubled by Love Excerpt

## Chapter 1

Amy He Metcalfe didn't believe in New Year's resolutions. January was no better month than any other to start changing your life. But four months ago, she had decided to focus a little more on her own goals, and when she was offered a job DC, she had said yes.

DC wasn't far from Philadelphia, where she had gone to college. It was a great opportunity, and her boyfriend Ryder traveled so much she'd see him about the same amount anyway.

She had not counted on finding herself pregnant of course.

Ryder: What time is the appointment?

Amy: 10 am

Amy held onto the phone for another second, but there were no more bubbles indicating he was texting back.

Ryder's job as emergency communications strategist kept him on the move. About six weeks ago, a sudden storm had him in town for an extra day, and they had run out of condoms. Their plans to just use hands and mouths had disappeared.

Amy purchased Plan B at the pharmacy the next day. But she had read all the fine print, and knew Plan B didn't work if you were already pregnant by the time you took it.

Amy knew a lot of stats about both contraception and abortion. She was the eldest of seven kids. Amy had bought her first pack of condoms at ten, placing them prominently at her mother's bedside.

Lots of siblings, especially female siblings knew a lot about middle of the night feedings, diaper changes, making lunches, or back to school shopping on an extreme budget. Amy had gotten any desire to raise kids out of her system well before the school sex ed program came to scare her about teen parenthood.

The sex ed program in Nevada suggested abstinence. Teen Amy had known she couldn't convince her mom of abstinence. Her mom never opened the condoms Amy bought her. The pill, in addition to being expensive, had turned out to have a terrible effect on her mom's depression.

Amy had discovered while she herself as an adult had not previously shown signs of depression, she inherited the same reaction to the pill. She and her ob/gyn had gone through a few of them, before her ob/gyn suggested that condoms had no such side effects. Plan B as a backup was probably better for her mental health.

All of this added up to Amy making a dreaded call to Ryder. She explained she was pregnant, she had an appointment to get the medication necessary to end the pregnancy. She didn't like ultimatums, but he could either get his butt back here or they were officially over. He had agreed to everything.

Then a hurricane hit the Caribbean. Amy had learned to hate hurricanes for many reasons - evidence of climate change, destruction wrought, but also because those bastards sent Ryder places without warning. Ryder should be off the schedule, of course, for the next few days.

Her phone rang and there was a knock on the door. Figuring Ryder had made it from the airport early, she threw open the door without looking, only to find an unfamiliar dark-haired, brown-eyed man standing there. "Next door," Amy said. Her neighbor had a lot of friends and often they knocked on her door by accident.

"Amy?" he said.

Amy stopped swinging the door closed. She knew better than to confirm her name to a stranger, but the folks looking for her neighbor Helena never knew her name.

Her phone chirped one more time and then went silent.

"I'm Dan," stranger dude said, "and I think that was Ryder calling to warn you. I made good time."

Amy wanted to slam the door now. It wasn't stranger dude's fault. Dan. Stranger dude's name was Dan. If Ryder had sent a stranger to her door, he wasn't on a plane. Not to here at least.

"Is it the hurricane?" Amy asked. It wasn't a question that would make sense to anyone who didn't know Ryder.

Dan shook his head. "Mudslide in Japan."

"So, Ryder sent you to what - spend the night?" Amy asked. Part of her, a stupid hopeful part, was still crushed that just this freaking once, Ryder hadn't taken himself off the schedule. He could. His other coworkers did. Amy was nothing if not an expert at looking strong when she was crushed inside.

"I think the idea was for us to chat a bit before tomorrow. To make it less awkward." Dan grimaced a bit, as if he realized the awkward train had long ago left the station.

"Darling," Helena said, leaning out of her door, long strawberry blonde hair loose. "As fascinating as this has all been, could you either let him in or kick him out. Any minute now, Mrs. Overgaard is going to email the whole building."

"Thanks, Helena," Amy said flatly.

Helena smiled and shut her door.

Helena was right though. The building was old enough that the soundproofing between apartments was good, but hallway conversations carried. Mrs. Overgaard often sent emails to everyone in the building reminding them of courtesy and decorum. "Come on in, I guess," Amy said.

Probably, Ryder's friend Dan wasn't a serial killer. And if he was, well, Amy didn't have a plan for that. Her plan for Ryder not showing up had been to go to the clinic herself. She'd been assured the pills were fairly painless, and had stocked up on super-strength pads, a bunch of microwave meals, and sports drinks. She had a streaming list of silly, lighthearted comedies, and dark revenge dramas, for her every mood.

She sat dead center on the couch, in her partially unpacked living room. Having to find the Planned Parenthood clinic her first week in DC had not been on her to do list. Nor had asking for a planned sick day before she'd had a chance to accrue any leave. Her boss had been great about it, made sure Amy had enough funds. But Amy had hoped that was it. That was enough awkward and uncomfortable at least for the month, but she should have known. The universe had endless wells of awkward and uncomfortable, and when it decided it was your turn, it was like a mudslide.

*\*\*\**

Dan Rees had known Ryder since they were teenagers. Dan had grown up in DC, and Ryder in Pennsylvania, but their families had both been Unitarian Universalists, and so they had met at a regional family summer camp for UUs. When his mom had gotten too sick to go, they had figured on missing a year. But the Rivette family had picked Dan up and let him stay in their cabin for the week so that Dan could get some fun in.

So, Dan had known Ryder long enough, the bond was deep enough, that when Ryder called and said, "Hey, my girlfriend has a medical procedure tomorrow, and I'm not going to make it. Could you go say hi, I'll clear it with her." - Dan had said okay.

Standing in Amy's living room, looking at her dark hair, yoga pants, and a t-shirt faded from several years of washings, he was rethinking this. Between Ryder and Dan's hectic schedules, he'd barely seen Ryder in person in the last few years. He'd heard about but never met Amy. Amy didn't seem to have any info about him.

Dan was torn between making an excuse to leave and hugging her. The dark circles under her eyes told him sleep had been hard to come by. Working as a rideshare driver to supplement his income while he awaited permit approval on his food truck, he knew what someone who'd been running themselves ragged looked like. So yeah, he was going to try to stay. At least long enough to convince her to let him drive her tomorrow.

She had plopped in the middle of the couch. Looking around the living room, he found a lone chair next to a small table and flipped it around to sit facing her.

"So, Ryder was calling you to tell you, but he and I go way back. I realize that doesn't fix the stranger to you part, but he did want to make sure you had someone with you tomorrow."

Dan had put two and two together and was pretty clear what type of medical appointment a woman would want her boyfriend taking her to. Ryder had sounded very apologetic on the phone, but Dan was sure that was very little comfort to Amy. Ryder and the Rivette family had been rocks for him and his dad. Dan was happy to return the favor, but this was not quite the same. However, he was sure at least not having to worry about transportation to the appointment was something he could help out with.

Amy picked up her phone and tossed it back down on the couch. "He's boarded the plane, but yeah, he says you'll do everything he would have done. Let's assume he didn't think that sentence all the way through."

Yeesh. Yeah. "Well, I make great soup, so if you tell me your favorite, I can bring some when I pick you up tomorrow."

"You don't have to pick me up just because Ryder told you you should," Amy said. "I'll be fine."

"I know," Dan said. "But please let me."

"I can call a cab or whatever."

"I technically am a cab or whatever, emphasis on the whatever," Dan said. "So think of it as saving a step."

"Okay."

They exchanged numbers, confirmed the time she wanted to leave, and Dan knew he should go. She may need to cry, scream, or do any other number of things it would be odd to do in front of a stranger.

"Oh, soup," he said.

"I bought a bunch of microwave thingies," Amy said, her hand waving in the direction of the fridge.

"I've got lentil, squash, and curried cauliflower in my freezer,." Dan said.

"Fine."

Dan nodded. "Do you have everything you need to get some sleep?"

"I'll be fine."

Dan nodded again and stood. "Okay, I'll see you tomorrow."

He paused in the hallway until he heard the lock click behind him, taking the stairs down a floor and out to his car. Amy's appointment tomorrow was late enough he'd hopefully be able to park right in front of the building.

He texted Ryder that he'd talked to Amy. It was a Wednesday night, so Xavier was unlikely to need him at the bar. He did text Xavier that he might not be available this weekend, sick friend. Dan wasn't on the schedule this week, but the others knew he would often pick up shifts if they needed backup.

He drove to the grocery store where he picked up a bunch of ingredients. He'd told Amy the truth, he had tons of soup in his freezer. But sometimes chicken ginger soup and maybe a baked potato soup were what you needed. Making soup tonight would give him time to think about what it meant that somehow his longtime friend Ryder's idea of a favor had turned into please take my girlfriend to the clinic to get an abortion.

***

Amy looked at the phone. Ryder's plane ride to Japan would take hours. They should have this conversation in person. Of course, his not being here was why they needed to have the conversation.

Amy: Stay safe in Japan. I told you if you couldn't take yourself off the schedule for me this one time, that was it. I meant it. Sending your friend doesn't count. So, we're done now.

Her finger hovered over the send button. Amy expected to feel something but she felt empty. Sometimes being the oldest sibling meant getting used to everyone else getting what they wanted first. Amy had hoped getting away, to college, to the East Coast, would help. Ryder was part of the pattern she needed to leave behind. She pressed send.

*More of* Troubled by Love *is available at various etailers and in print. More info here:* www.tarakennedy.com/books[1]

---

1. http://www.tarakennedy.com/books

# Don't miss out!

Visit the website below and you can sign up to receive emails whenever Tara Kennedy publishes a new book. There's no charge and no obligation.

https://books2read.com/r/B-A-GUVI-MJBDD

**BOOKS 2 READ**

Connecting independent readers to independent writers.

Milton Keynes UK
Ingram Content Group UK Ltd.
UKHW022309040624
443649UK00001B/115